Something In The Dark

RUNNING HORSE

DEDICATION

This book is dedicated to victory over our fears
and to Val (Cherokee) my fearless friend.

Something In The Dark

Pamela Cowan

And God saw the light, that it was good,
and God divided the light from the darkness.
Genesis 1:4

PROLOGUE

Building No. 246, US Army Family Housing,
Pattonville, West Germany

"I don't want to play," Austin said.

"Sure you do," her brother, Muncie, insisted. "Come on. All you have to do is sit inside, right here in this spot," he patted the ground inside the doorway, obliterating the tic-tac-toe game she'd drawn in the dirt earlier. "We'll shut the door and the lights will come on. You just have to look around and see what's in there. Then, after we count to ten, we'll open the door and let you out and you'll tell us what you saw."

"You promise you'll open it right back up?" Austin asked.

"We promise," said Muncie and his friend Brian, both solemnly crossing the area above their hearts.

"And you promise you'll play hopscotch?" she asked doubtfully.

"We promise," said the boys.

"Well, okay," she agreed reluctantly, glaring at them to

let them know they'd better.

Austin let them half-lift, half-push her through the doorway. The dirt floor was soft and powdery. It made her sneeze.

While the boys went back to work unwinding the wire that held the door open, Austin began clearing away the bits of rubbish around her, tossing empty soda bottles and crumpled bits of newspaper deeper into the impenetrable maw of the hole in the wall.

The place was really creepy and dirty. Maybe she should tell them she'd changed her mind, that they didn't have to bother untwisting the rest of the wire.

It was too late. The weight of the huge metal door finished the job for them. The strands sprang apart with a hissing sound, one sharp end slicing Brian's cheek. Then, the door slammed shut with a sound like thunder that echoed down the long hallway.

Austin gasped, shocked by the noise and the sudden darkness. Immediately she began to count. "One, two, three." She couldn't hear anything. Were they there? "Four, five, six." She didn't hear them moving, or counting, or anything. "Seven, eight, nine, ten." Well, maybe she was counting too fast. She counted again–then again.

She started to get angry. Creeps. Boys were creeps. They liked to push you down, and break your things, and tell lies about you. She wouldn't ever play with them again. They probably weren't even really going to play hopscotch. They only said that so she'd sit in this dark, dirty hole. There weren't any lights. There wasn't any secret room. It was all a big fat lie. If they lied about that–maybe they lied about letting her out too.

She blinked her eyes. Were her eyes open? She thought they were, but it was so dark they must be closed. Putting her hands to her face, she felt her eyelids quiver.

Open or closed, the dark was just the same. She felt the dampness at the corners of her eyes. They were tears, but she wasn't ready to cry, at least not just yet. She was a big girl, after all. She counted again.

"One, two." What if they didn't come back? Her mom would be mad. Her dad would be mad too. They would ask her brother where she was. But what if her brother was afraid to say? What if he thought he'd get in trouble if he told them she was in the hole-in-the-wall? What if he never told anybody? She cried a little bit. It made her feel better. Then a new thought struck.

Maybe her mom and dad would think she was strangulated, like that girl on the television that she heard her daddy say got kidnapped, and strangulated, and dead. That girl was six years old. Horrible things happened to children nowadays. That's what her mom and dad said. Horrible things like getting put in holes.

Crouched, shivering in the dark, Austin knocked on the heavy iron door until her knuckles ached and she had to stop. At least the pain was a distraction, a reassurance that there was something other than darkness, even if she was too young to put those feelings into words. After awhile, not knowing what else to do, she knocked on the door again, first rapping with her knuckles, then with her balled fists, and finally, with the palms of her hands. Smack, smack went her hands. Just like patty cake. Slap, slap, slap.

She pressed her face against the door. It was icy cold against her flushed, tear-streaked face. "Mommy. Mommy," she called. "I'm in here. I'm right in here."

No one heard. Minutes that seemed like hours later, Austin's throat was sore, her voice a raw, rasping whisper. She was exhausted–with a deep, ragged breath she sank to the floor. She pressed herself against the door, as close to outside as she could get. Without thought, her thumb slipped into her mouth, a habit she had outgrown by the time she was three. She closed her eyes and did the only thing left–she waited.

After awhile, once her heart had slowed and her sobs had subsided to an occasional hiccup, she began to hear-- something. It was a very small noise. She only seemed able to catch it in between breaths. She held her breath to see if she could hear it. Yes, there it was. It sounded like–like someone breathing.

Austin's eyes flew wide with alarm. She took a long but shallow breath and held it. She heard it again. Someone *was* breathing. Someone–or something–was in here with her. Maybe it had always been here, hiding in the shadows where the light couldn't reach. Maybe it was a man, the man who made that girl dead. Maybe it was a big rat. Muncie had a fake rubber rat. It was creepy, with its long naked, whippy tail and its fat pointy teeth. He was always throwing it on her lap so she would jump up and yell.

"Rats will eat your face off," Muncie had told her. "Bite off your nose and eat your eyeballs."

Austin put her hands over her face. From her small, strained throat came tiny, broken whimpers.

"No they won't", her mom had told her. "Your brother is teasing you." But moms lied. Moms told you shots didn't hurt, and if you're nice to him your brother won't pick on you, and your dad will be home in time to tell you a bedtime story. Still, she would give anything if her mom would come soon. But her mom didn't.

Chapter 1

Nineteen years later, on a dark autumn morning, Austin heard the hinges on the front gate squeal. The sound sent a shiver down her spine. She shook off the sensation irritably. She wasn't that little girl anymore. Those hours spent in darkness were far behind, and yet the scars of that day continued to haunt her. The sound of a shutting door, a closed space such as an elevator and worst of all, finding herself in the dark, were all triggers that sent her into the same mindless panic.

Well, there was nothing sinister about hearing her own front gate. All it meant was that Josh, one of her employees, had arrived. She swallowed the rest of her coffee and shrugged into her flannel-lined rain jacket.

Looking out through the picture window, she noted how gray the sky was, clouds heavy with rain or snow. The sun seemed to rise more slowly than usual, as if the haze of mist was too heavy to push away.

She decided it was going to be a miserably cold day. Well, there wasn't a thing she could do about it. She screwed down the top of the thermos she'd earlier filled with scalding, heavily sugared coffee, grabbed her leather gloves, the ring of keys from the table, and opened the door.

She thought of inviting Josh inside to warm up, but knew the earlier they got started the earlier they'd get done.

Josh was chaining his mountain bike to a gatepost, a stocking cap pulled over his ears, his cheeks red from the wind and his ride. Faded jeans encased long slender legs and the layers of turtleneck, flannel shirt, and corduroy jacket made him look bulkier than he was. Pale fingers struggled with the padlock, but he persisted, fumbling with it until finally it snapped into place.

"I don't know why you do that," Austin said. "It's not like anyone will steal it. You're not in the big city anymore, Dorothy."

"That's Toto to you," he replied, giving the padlock a tug to be sure it was locked. "Anyway, you trust people too much."

"Well, you make up for it by not trusting them at all. For a nineteen-year-old, you do a great imitation of a very cynical and paranoid old man."

Josh didn't disagree. They looked up at the sound of a truck clattering down the winding road that curved past Austin's house. Cars went by Austin's rather isolated house occasionally, but it was only seven o'clock.

Austin said, "It must be Paco." You could set your watch by her foreman's arrival. Sometimes she actually wished Paco weren't so prompt. It made it hard to pretend she was the driving force behind the success of Blue Spruce Landscaping.

He pulled in and parked his truck alongside hers. During the summer Austin hired extra help and ran three crews, using both of her pickups and Paco's. It was getting close to snow season, lawns were going dormant, so they were only working out of one truck and getting by with one crew made up of Paco, Josh and, on their heaviest days, Austin.

Paco strode across the driveway, carrying his lunch pail in one hand, a pair of heavy leather work gloves in the other. "Good morning," he greeted them both. Are we ready to go?"

"We're ready." Austin said. She unlocked the truck's passenger door, and Paco climbed in and slid to the middle of the bench seat. Josh climbed in beside him and Austin walked around and got in on the driver's side. As she started the pickup she said, "I hope I can remember how to back this thing up."

No one responded. They were used to her morning mantra. She put the truck in reverse and twisted to see behind her as she backed it, and the long trailer full of landscaping equipment, out of the wide driveway.

"Damn it's cold," Josh said, rubbing his hands together. He reached across Paco and turned on the heater.

"There he goes again," said Austin. "You think he'll ever learn?"

"Not likely," said Paco. "Every morning I have the frozen wind on my knees because Josh cannot wait."

"Ahh, bunch of whiners," said Josh, still rubbing his hands together. It'll keep the window from frosting up."

Austin shivered. Since buying the nursery, she hadn't worked the lawn maintenance side of the business very often. Thursday mornings, and when she covered for someone who was out sick, were about the only times that she got away from the store.

The steering wheel was icy, and because the truck's engine hadn't warmed up yet, so was the steady blast of air from the heater. Being uncomfortable was no surprise to any of them. For the next six to ten hours they would be at the mercy of the weather. They would probably freeze, roast, get soaking wet, or all three. By the end of any given day they were also guaranteed to have new blisters, scratches, bruises, bug bites, bee stings, and calluses.

Austin's neatly brushed hair, dark chestnut, with sun-bleached copper strands, was currently twisted into a smooth tight bun at the back of her neck. By day's end it would be a loose, lopsided knot with stray strands twisted around it and wisps standing on end. Her faded jeans would be grass-stained and speckled with the heavy clay mud that would also cover her steel-toed boots. She would be tired, sore, dirty, and hungry.

She missed it. Some days she wished she hadn't bought the nursery and that she could just keep on forever working outside, not just watching the seasons change but feeling it on her skin and in her bones. Of course a lot of people would argue that working in a nursery *was* working outside, but Austin wouldn't have agreed. She felt she spent far too much time in the office dealing with paperwork, or in the sheds and green houses, closed in, while she planted the flowers that would grace someone's yard.

And then there was the camaraderie. An old-fashioned word, but one she felt justified in using. She missed the shared sense of accomplishment that comes after a day of hard labor, not to mention the water fights, the practical jokes, and the Saturday barbecues, complete with beer and lying contests. Sometimes she even missed the salty, tangy smell of sweat and herbicide that filled the cab of the truck.

They drove toward one of Austin's favorite parts of

town, a somewhat rural area that held average ranch-style homes, most nicely kept, painted in muted shades and sitting on plots of land measured in acres instead of feet. Here and there, a fenced field held a pony or a small herd of goats. There were fruit trees and vegetable gardens, turned and bare for the winter. Somewhere nearby, a rooster crowed.

They arrived at the first job of the day. The yard was a quarter acre of stubby grass surrounded by fir trees and dotted with irregular flowerbeds. It belonged to one of Austin's favorite customers, Granny Birdie.

Austin was grateful that Granny's driveway was straight, and deep enough to pull both the truck and trailer completely off the road. Without needing to speak, the three climbed out of the truck.

Paco and Josh lowered the ramp on the trailer, then Paco drove the riding mower off the back and onto the front lawn. He lowered the blade to the height Granny preferred and began cutting neat swathes. Josh pushed one of two mowers down the ramp and began to mow between the flowerbeds and anywhere else the riding mower wouldn't fit.

Austin climbed into the trailer and unhooked the bungee cord that held the gas-powered trimmer against one of the wooden side rails. She rested it on the ramp, pumped some gas into the carburetor, set the choke, and pulled the start cord three times. As always, the dependable machine came to life with an almost bloodthirsty eagerness. Austin put on the goggles that had been hooked around the machine's handle. She fished a set of earplugs out of the pocket of her flannel shirt, twisted them in place, dulling the roar of machinery, and set to work.

Soon the rhythmic action, sidestep, sweep, sidestep,

and the smell of freshly cut grass lulled Austin into a state of pure relaxation. This, she knew, was as close to bliss as you could reach. This was a state of disconnection that was pure connection. Zen and the art of mowing lawns.

Austin and Paco finished at almost the same moment. Josh took one last swipe around the yard's perimeter, picking up whatever stray cuttings Austin's trimmer had left on the lawn. It was this attention to detail that had made Austin's business grow at such a phenomenal rate—at least that's what she believed.

She would never have entertained the notion that it was her kindness to her customers, the patience she showed in taking the time to hear what they had to say, that convinced them to tell their friends and neighbors about her. The fact that she looked damn good in a pair of cutoff shorts and a tank top didn't hurt either. If she'd had any inkling that she'd sometimes been hired because someone was willing to pay to watch her work, she would have been more amused than offended. She had lost a few jobs because she was "just" a woman. She would have been more than willing to pick up a few for the same reason.

Austin pushed the goggles onto her forehead and rubbed at the red mark they always left on the bridge of her nose. She handed her trimmer to Josh and, as he and Paco put the equipment away, removed the earplugs and climbed the wide steps to Granny's front door.

Chapter 2

Before Austin could knock, Granny opened the door. "First things first," she said with a wide grin. She held a check out to Austin. Only after it was safely folded and in Austin's pocket did Granny continue. "So, what'll it be? I've got zucchini bread or ginger snaps."

"Now Granny, you know you don't have to keep baking for us."

"Honey, I don't bake for you. I bake for me. I only pretend I bake for you." Granny slapped her denim-clad thigh and laughed.

Austin couldn't help but laugh too. Granny had that affect on her. Like everything about her, Granny's laugh was special, so full of life and freely expressed that Austin couldn't help but join in.

Despite her age which, based on her stories, must be in the eighties at least, Granny was one of the most actively alive people Austin had ever met.

Her hair was smoky gray, with just a few shiny, silver strands. She kept it gathered in a thick-braided coil at the back of her neck. Austin was sure that, brushed out, it would reach the floor. Her skin was baby thin and crisscrossed with wrinkles, especially around her mouth and the corners of her eyes. She invariably wore brightly colored blouses tucked into men's jeans, which were turned up at the hems, and ironed so they held a razor- sharp crease. Over that she wore a bib apron in bleached white linen, its innumerable pockets bulging with an ever-changing assortment of objects.

"Some of both, I think, cookies and bread," Granny said after she'd finished laughing and caught her breath. "Now you sit down there and take a little break."

"No time, Granny. We have a lot of work today."

"You have a lot of work every day. Trust me honey. Work is something a body never runs short of. Your boys will want to have their smoke. Sit you down while I get those cookies and fetch my pipe. Sit, and mind your elders."

"Yes ma'am," Austin sat down in one of the two Adirondack chairs on Granny's narrow front porch. Granny was right, of course. Paco and Josh had finished loading the truck and were leaning against it talking and lighting up.

Granny returned with a plastic bread wrapper full of cookies and foil-wrapped packages of zucchini bread. Austin, who'd had her usual two cups of coffee and nothing else for breakfast, took the bag gratefully. Granny tapped her corncob pipe on the porch rail. She took a sack of tobacco from a pocket of her apron then filled, tamped, and lit her pipe. She took her first puff then sat in the chair beside Austin with a contented sigh.

"My husband showed me how to smoke. I was curious, you see. Women weren't allowed to smoke then, least not in public. He didn't think that was fair and . . .

Austin found her mind wandering, as she heard the now familiar story, but politely forced herself to be attentive.

". . . and I would sneak out in the woods and have a few puffs," Granny continued. "Once we got married I didn't have to sneak, and it wasn't near as fun. Nothing ever is as much fun as sneakin' and gettin' away with it. Ask any politician."

Austin smiled. Sometimes, when Granny told stories about her early life in Virginia, she would lapse into a sort of singsong, her accent, words and phrases becoming pure hill country. At other times she would speak with the clarity and enunciation of the most pretentious English professor. Strangely, neither seemed more or less appropriate for her. They were both just part of who she was.

"Thank you for the cookies, Granny," Austin said, preparing to stand. "I think the guys are about ready to go, and as much as I'd like to stay and visit, it gets dark early these days."

"Austin, I'm an old lady," Granny said, reaching out to pat Austin's hand. "Some of the neighbors think I'm a bit queer. Sometimes I think they might be right. But I've seen a lot of things and I'm not one to question them. I'm a Christian, have been all my life. I know that sometimes signs are sent to us. Why and how this is I don't know. But, last night I had a dream." Granny continued, "It was very strong and it stayed with me after I woke. I've had those kinds of dreams a few times, and sometimes they come true. Oh, not chapter and verse, but the sense of them, the feeling you get from them. Well, it's hard to explain. The reason I'm telling you all this is because the dream was about you."

Granny had Austin's full attention now.

"You were at the side of some water," Granny continued. "Don't know if it was lake or river. Pretty sure not ocean 'cause there was no waves, but I could be wrong. You were sitting there, beside that water. The moon was out. Must have been night. The moon was biggest I've ever seen. Big and bright and the stars, thousands of them, and all the way to the horizon you could see them. It was like you were sitting inside an upside-down bowl, painted with stars, and the moon over your shoulder like. You were sitting there on the ground and water all around you, dark it was and deep.

"Then I seen how it was creeping up on you, getting higher all-round. I tried to yell out, to warn you to tuck your feet in. Crazy, like most dreams are, me not wanting you to get your feet wet. You were sitting there looking straight up at the sky, not giving no mind to the water 'cause see, them stars, they was going out, one after another and then two at a time, three at a time, four. . .

"So you didn't see that water, though it come up and touched you, sort of seeped up around you. You must have felt it finally 'cause you reached down and brushed at it, like a body might brush away a bug that had lit on em. Only your fingers went into that water and when you pulled them out they were all black, like you'd dipped them into an ink well. You got this look on your face. Lord, I never seen such a look. You were scared. So afraid of that blackness on your fingers and that water was coming up fast, climbing over your ankles, your calves, your knees, and you opened your mouth to scream and I woke up screaming for you.

"That scream," Granny said, with a self-conscious laugh, "nearly scared my old tomcat to death."

For a moment Austin sat there speechless. She'd been so caught up in the dream that her heart was actually pounding. Shaking it off, she looked at Granny and said, "That sounds horrible, but it was only a bad dream."

"A bad dream for certain, sure. It made me feel all jittery, and I got up and had some warm milk and a touch of that gin you kids picked up for me."

Granny knocked her pipe out against the edge of the porch. "Well, that's all I had to say. Maybe it wasn't nothing. Maybe it was a warning to you. Either way, you be careful today, and take care with that equipment you use."

"I'll be careful," Austin promised.

Chapter 3

Austin had divided her lawn maintenance territory into five sections of Blue Spruce: the North Hills, the Heights, The South Hills, Lakeshore, and downtown. Her crews worked in a different area each day of the week.

Today was Thursday, so they were in the South Hills, a semi-rural area of older homes and small farms. Most residents there keep a few cows or a horse, chickens and almost always a garden or remnants of an orchard.

Both Austin's house and her nursery were located in the South Hills, her nursery near the base of the hills and her house a couple miles further up a winding gravel road.

Austin had moved to the town after college, lured to the area by a desire to live near her best friend, and kept there by the beauty of the county.

Near the center of Oregon, in the Southwest corner of Eulalona County is the town of Blue Spruce. The town sits in a fir and pine-studded valley that's part of the Cascade Mountain Range. Austin had been fascinated by the topography of the area ever since noticing on a map how much the valley resembled a hand, with the palm flat and the fingers pointing east.

She kept that map in mind when dividing up her lawn maintenance territory.

At the wrist of the valley is the Lakeshore, a neighborhood of homes whose docks lead from manicured back lawns to the dark blue of Sapphire Lake. These are the homes of people who love to sail and Jet Ski, and who can afford to pay for the privilege.

To the north is a low range of hills that hold most of the area's gravel factories and lumber mills. Homes in this area are smaller but just as well-kept by their owners.

To the east, at the tips of the fingers, are The Heights, another range of hills, but twisted and crumpled like the sheets on a giant's unkempt bed. Here, on torturously winding streets with breathtaking views of the valley, are the homes of the town's most prosperous homeowners. Driving the truck with its trailer up the long switchbacks, and finding a place to turn around, not to mention mowing up and down steep hills, was challenging for Austin and her crews. Fortunately the residents were able to pay well for their lawn care, and Austin was well compensated for the effort.

The actual town of Blue Spruce, shortened to Spruce by the locals, takes up only a small grid of a dozen streets at the base of The Heights, right where the first and second fingers join. The palm of the hand is potato farms and cattle ranches and miles and miles of hay fields. Austin rarely worked for farmers. They had their own equipment and the do-it-yourself attitude that could put her out of business.

Two main rivers meander from the north and south corners of The Heights to empty into Sapphire Lake, neatly dividing the valley into thirds. The Diamond in the north is used by the lumber mills and is brown, polluted with mud and silt. The Broken River, which dives underground for a few miles and then bubbles back up, just past the town limits, is loaded with native fish and clean enough for swimming.

Austin was looking forward to Saturday and the canoe trip on Broken River she'd planned with her best friend, Janice. The clouds and cold would not bother Janice, who was a native of the high altitude Oregon Cascades and knew how to dress for the ever-changing weather.

They left Granny's house, and it was only a short drive to their next work site. The South Hills day was usually an easy one, the lawns large enough for the tractor and flat. The rest of the day saw them moving from one job to another with no more interruptions or delays.

The wind began to pick up around two in the afternoon, and a cold mix of rain and sleet began to fall. They zipped up their raincoats and pulled up their hoods. Still, even though they were familiar with unpredictable weather and had dressed well, nothing could completely protect them from the numbing cold. The gray sky grew ever darker and Austin began thinking again about Granny's equally dark dream.

Stamping her feet to warm them, Austin started trimming out the last of the yards. Back and forth, back and forth. Dark waters climbing up around her. What a strange dream. Maybe Granny's dream had only foretold what a lousy day it was going to be.

To make things worse she was getting wet to the skin. She'd caught her raincoat on a nail in the back of the truck and now there was a long tear in it under one arm. She'd have to sew it. It was a new coat, so no sense even thinking about throwing it away and buying a new one, and if there was anything she hated more than sewing she didn't know what. Didn't matter. No way could she afford to just throw things away, not when she had to come up with enough money to get the roof on the second greenhouse fixed. Stupid dream. So maybe she did feel like she was drowning sometimes. She wasn't, not really. Just wanting it all to happen right away. That was her problem.

She swept the machine back and forth, getting some enjoyment from decapitating the seed-heavy heads of the grass. Off with their heads. Off with their heads. Her mood began to shift. She even managed a small smile. The pity party is officially over, she thought. She shut off the machine and put it away, then retrieved the check from the place where almost everybody left it, under the front doormat. By the time she came back with it, Josh was sitting on the back of the truck, lighting his post-lawn cigarette while Paco was tying down the mower. The back of the truck was full of grass clippings.

"Come on," she said. "You can smoke in the truck. I'm too tired to wait for you, and too cold to complain."

"All right," said Josh enthusiastically, and he held the door, waiting for Paco.

Austin left her window open several inches to let the smoke out, but she had been telling the truth, she was too cold to worry about such trifling things as lung cancer or emphysema. All she cared about, at the moment, was getting home and taking a hot shower.

She drove too fast up the winding road that climbed into the north hills to the county landfill. The man inside the small shack at the gate waved her through without asking for payment. He extended this courtesy once in a while to his frequent customers, usually landscapers or construction crews. She waved and mouthed a 'Thank you' as she drove past and up to the steaming pile of grass clippings they had been adding to all summer.

Josh jumped out of the truck and unhitched the trailer. As soon as he was through, Austin swung the pickup around and backed to the edge of the grass hill. Before she had even come to a complete stop, Josh was jumping into the back and reaching for a pitchfork. She and Paco climbed out of the truck and helped him unload the sodden, heavily compacted pile of grass. This was her least favorite part of the day. Not only did the landfill have its usual knee-buckling aroma, but grass, sitting under sun and rain and baking into a bacterially active stew, smells nothing like a newly mown lawn. Still, better to get rid of it today, because time did nothing to improve the stench. It took only a few minutes to fork, shovel and sweep the pickup clean. In a short while they had hitched up the trailer and were bumping down the landfill road. As soon as they cleared the gate, Josh lit a cigarette.

"Just killing the smell," he said in response to her disapproving look.

She shook her head, but didn't say any more. She had to be careful that the people she hired didn't think they could get away with murder. She knew she had a tendency to be too friendly with her employees. More than once Paco had warned her that it wasn't such a good idea.

"They will think you are weak. They will try little things to test you and then they will try bigger things, and soon who will have the business? Not you."

"It's your fault," she had responded. "You spoil me. I reach for something, you put it in my hand. I wonder if I remembered to do something, you say you've taken care of it. You are the best employee I ever had, and if you ever quit me, I will devote myself to making your life miserable."

"I understand entirely well. When is my raise?"

"Ha. When is mine?"

So, was Josh testing her to see if she'd enforce the "no smoking in the truck" ban, or had he assumed that since she let them smoke on the way to the landfill that it was all right? Should she say something? Should she let it go? Was this the sort of problem that drove so many CEOs to drink? She smiled at the thought and decided to let it go. She didn't have the energy to challenge Josh – at the moment.

They pulled into the wide driveway beside Austin's house and Austin cleaned out the cab of the pickup, removing the empty soda cans and trash from lunch. Josh pulled a hose into the trailer and washed down the equipment, sending a green stream of water and grass clippings down the driveway. From there it flowed into a culvert, cheaply constructed of fifty gallon drums laid end to end, that carried the sluggish runoff to an irrigation ditch. It was part of a system meant to carry water to the hay fields behind the house, but Austin had yet to decide whether she was going to try to grow hay herself or rent the use of the land to one of her farming neighbors. It was just another decision she would have to think about. But not tonight. Paco topped off the gas tanks, added oil to the trimmer mixture and made sure all the equipment was secured. That done, they were ready for the next day's work. As they were finishing, the yard-light at the corner of the garage hummed noisily and blinked on.

"Holy shit, I think I'm blind." Josh said, dramatically throwing his arm across his eyes.

Austin grinned at his theatrics. "It's not that bright."

"Are you kidding? Tell the truth, how often do ships try to dock here? Do the airplanes landing in the yard keep you awake all night?"

"Not one bit, it seems" she said, holding her hand in front of her mouth as she yawned. You two are going to meet here in the morning and work Snob Hill, er, The Heights tomorrow, right?"

"Yes," said Paco.

"OK. I'll check the phone for messages and if anyone has canceled, or anything has changed, I'll stick a note on the front door before I leave for the nursery. Oh, and don't forget to tie up the O'Brian's arborvitaes tomorrow. If we get an early snow and they get bent out of shape the O'Brians are going to be extremely unhappy, especially since they've already called and reminded me twice this week."

"I won't forget," Paco promised.

"Yeah, I've seen Mr. O'Brian bent out of shape before. Not pretty," offered Josh, grinning.

`"You want a ride home?" Paco asked him, not getting the play on words.

"Nah, it'd take longer to load the bike than to just ride there. I'll see you in the morning."

Josh unlocked his bike and, with a final cigarette hanging defiantly from his lip, pedaled out of the driveway and turned right, heading for his parent's house just on the other side of the hill behind Austin's place.

Paco climbed into his pickup, backed out, and headed in the opposite direction, toward town and his waiting wife and two young children.

Austin felt the emptiness left by their departure and hurried into the house. Suddenly the wide fields, with their deep shadows, seemed like perfect hiding places for all kinds of unimaginable things. Once inside, she locked the door behind her and sighed with relief. She knew her night fears were ridiculous but she could no sooner control them than she could the weather.

Dinner or shower first was her next concern. She hung her coat on a hook to drip dry on the patch of linoleum just inside the door. Then she sat on the bench that had been placed there for the same reason, to spare the carpet, and unknotted the wet laces on her boots with some difficulty. She curled and flexed her toes and sighed. Shower first—a nice, long, hot shower.

Moments later Austin was standing under a blast of water so hot it turned her skin bright red. She closed her eyes and sighed as she got truly warm for the first time in hours. She shampooed her hair, making a face when she found a cluster of grass seed tangled there. Very attractive, she thought, I wonder how long that's been there.

She finished washing her hair and combed conditioner through it with her fingers. Next she rubbed a bar of ivory soap over her bath sponge and began to scrub her skin. Tiny cuts on her fingers stung but she ignored them. She ran the sponge around her neck and down her arms, then over her breasts and across her stomach. She noted with some detachment that her body looked great, not a bit of fat anywhere. A nice dividend for having a physically demanding job, she reminded herself.

Not that it was that demanding lately. She had two people working the landscaping business and two at the nursery. Four people counting on her for their paychecks was what it meant. It had happened so slowly: needing some extra help, she'd hired Paco, and then Josh. Then buying the nursery, and that meant another two people and then she got too busy at the nursery and Paco needed help, so there were the part-timers in the summer.

Austin shook her head and fought off a wave, first of wonder and then of fear. How had she managed to become responsible for the livelihoods of other people? It was crazy. Thinking about it was disturbing, so she would quit thinking about it. She turned her thoughts to Blake.

Blake, now there was a nice distraction. She'd met him barely a week ago, when he walked into the nursery with a map open in his hands. He'd said he was lost. That he was supposed to be meeting a real estate agent to look at some ranch property. She gave him directions. First pointing out his destination and then, at his urging, using a yellow highlighter to draw the route on the map. Bent over the map, intent on what she was doing, she'd suddenly realized how close he was standing. Close enough to smell the clean citrus scent of his cologne. Close enough to make it hard to catch her breath.

Blake was tall and lean and everything about him, from his longish blond hair, green eyes, sweat-stained cowboy hat, tight jeans, and Toni Lama boots appealed to her. As her brother Muncie often accused, since moving to Blue Spruce she had indeed "gone native," and the Marlboro man ads were not lost on her. This man could easily have been the model for one of those ads. At five foot eight, she was used to standing at least close to eye- level with most men. That she actually had to look up at him stirred something in her stomach that she knew was primeval and silly, but impossible to ignore.

He talked to her in an easy, friendly way, as if they'd known each other before and were just catching up. He said he'd been working for different ranchers and saving up for a place of his own when suddenly he inherited a respectable sum of money from an aunt he had never even met. He liked the area and wanted to buy a ranch, raise some cattle, maybe grow some hay.

She thought part of her attraction to Blake was simply the recognition of how similar their stories were. She too had been working hard, learning a profession, when she had received an inheritance. It had changed her life as well.

He asked her to go out with him sometime, show him the countryside.

"After all, you know the area," he'd said, "Take pity on a guy who can't even read a map. Of course, I can understand you not wanting to drive around the county with a total stranger. So that's why I think we should get to know each other, over dinner?"

The invitation had been so unexpected she'd been too surprised to reply. Dumbstruck, she'd said nothing. It would have become awkward, but fortunately she was distracted by a lucky interruption--a customer's question.

By the time she was free again, he had gone. She was more than a little annoyed at herself for not saying yes when she had the chance. She was also relieved. And that was the way it had stayed. One minute she was mad at herself for being such a socially inept loser, and the next relieved that she hadn't become involved in something that would probably have ended up messy and painful.

That had seemed the best way to leave things--no regrets, nothing lost. Then he called the nursery and left a message for her. She hadn't called back. Not calling back was the same as saying 'No'. 'No' was okay, she decided, but then again, 'Yes' might have been nice, too. What an idiot! He was a gorgeous cowboy who smelled incredible and how often did you find that combination?

Austin ran the sponge across her breasts again, amused at how hard her nipples had become. Maybe she should try to think of something else. But the sponge felt so good, and when she slid her free hand down past her slippery stomach to the ache growing there, well that felt good too.

When she finally stepped out of the shower she was warm, relaxed and starving. She wrapped a towel around her head, put on her big, white, terry cloth robe and padded barefoot into the kitchen.

The kitchen had an alcove with a built-in desk and shelves. The space had probably been designed for paying bills and keeping cookbooks, but it had become her home office. The desk held her computer, a phone, an adding machine and stacks of paper waiting to be filed. The shelves were stuffed with books on plants and their diseases and magazine clippings of articles related to lawn maintenance.

As she walked past she pushed the button on the old-fashioned answering machine that had come with the house. Then she reached into the refrigerator for the lamb chops she'd left to thaw.

There were three messages. The first was a Ms. Teal looking for someone to mow her lawn. Austin took a moment to grab a pen and jot down her number and then deleted the message. The second message was from a current customer, Mr. Emerson, letting her know he and his wife were going out of town and wanted a fall cleanup and their shrubs tied. She wrote a note to herself to remind the guys to tie up bushes for all the customers. Snow would be falling soon, she thought as she reached over and deleted the message.

The last message was from Blake. His voice, so soon after her shower, made her blush. "I've decided three times must be the charm. How about dinner? You name the day. Or lunch if dinner won't work. I won't mention breakfast, since that might cause you to believe I have ideas. On the other hand, if breakfast would suit, well, call me." He left his number. How had he found her home number? Dumb question. It was listed. How clever, that ability to use a phone book. Bemused at that thought, as well as by the effect his voice had on her, she decided right then that she would say 'Yes' to dinner. She pressed the save button. Unaware that she was humming softly to herself, Austin took garlic from a hanging basket and began to chop it to cook with the lamb.

Chapter 4

On Friday morning Austin helped Bunny, the young woman she employed as a clerk, with the routine of opening the nursery store. Bunny counted the till and slipped the drawer into the register while Austin opened the sliding glass front doors and began carting out the merchandise they displayed in front.

Bunny was uncharacteristically quiet, but Austin was grateful. She had a lot on her mind, and all she wanted was a cup of coffee and some time to sort things out. Quarterly tax time was approaching. She had to figure out a way to keep everyone working during the winter months. The trucks needed tune-ups. But the problem foremost on her mind at the moment was how she would find the courage to return Blake's phone call and accept his invitation.

Austin measured coffee and poured it into the filter waiting in the coffee maker. She filled the machine from a garden hose hanging on the wall and pushed the on-button. The shelves are dusty, she thought as the coffee pot began to hiss and pop, and how much would it cost to knock out a wall and expand twenty feet or so?

The nursery, named Grace Gardens after Austin's mother, was situated on a little over 40 acres of nearly level ground. It was located just off the main highway, which cut through the south hills, then curved slightly east on its way through the valley and on to the north.

In addition to ten acres of cultivated fields, the nursery consisted of two large greenhouses, two small greenhouses, several outbuildings, a pump house and the store. This was a square building no larger than a two-car garage. Opposite the sliding doors, taking up a back corner, was an L-shaped counter. The long part of the L held the register. The short section held a coffeepot, cups, sugar, creamer and a tin of cookies that customers had to pass on their way in and out the back door. Behind the counter, along the back wall, a narrow table, with file cabinets for legs, held a computer, fax machine, phone and stacks of invoices. This was the office.

Austin had placed signs along the highway to attract tourists, and in the belief that tourists by nature would be more interested in unique finds than in gardening supplies, she had added the work of several local artists and craftsmen to the store. These hand-thrown pots, ceramic sculptures and carved bits of wood fought for space with racks of seeds, rolls of twine and cans of pesticide. Up above, across the open ceiling rafters, wire had been strung and hanging plants, mostly poinsettias at this time of year, filled nearly every inch of space. The store was a well-organized, if crowded, chaos of colors and textures.

As Austin was turning the "Open" sign around, she looked through the sliding glass doors and saw the other nursery employee, Will, walking across the parking lot. She opened the door for him. As he stepped inside Bunny snapped, "Nice of you to join us."

"Huh?" said Will.

"I said," repeated Bunny with a huge sigh, "How nice of you to join us."

"You are one sarcastic bitch, you know that?"

"Hey," said Austin, surprised and annoyed by their immediate hostility. "That is really not appropriate."

"She should get off my back."

"And maybe you should get to work on time," snapped Bunny.

"Okay, I don't know what is going on with you two and I don't really care. Just work it out somewhere else," Austin insisted.

"Uh-huh," Will mumbled under his breath, then, "I'll be out back potting up those bulbs that came in Tuesday."

"Good. That'll be fine."

After he'd gone Austin turned to Bunny. "So, what's going on?"

"Oh, he's such a jerk. He walks around with that long hair and that scraggly thing he calls a beard, pretending to be some kind of hippy."

"Well it takes all kinds, you know."

"I don't mind the hippie thing. It's just that he's such a phony. Do you know he has the key to a Mercedes on a chain around his neck?"

"No, I didn't, but so what?"

"Come on. Hippies aren't supposed to be into material things. It's proof of what a phony he is."

"Well, he works hard and is great with plants, and that's all I care about."

"Yeah, you don't know the half of it."

"What's that supposed to mean?"

"Oh, nothing. I'm just in a bad mood this morning, I guess."

"Fine."

Austin knew there was more going on than Bunny was willing to confess, at least to her boss, but she wasn't about to pry. She had a good idea what the problem was anyway. Bunny was–well, Bunny.

She had white blonde hair, big blue eyes and a heart-shaped face, but it wasn't her face that was her problem. It was her body. "Like a toothpaste tube squeezed in the middle," someone had once described it.

She was short, with heavy breasts and hips but a tiny waist. Austin didn't completely understand it, but the combination obviously worked, as men fell all over themselves trying to get close to Bunny. And the truth was, they really didn't have to try that hard. Bunny loved the attention. Austin knew the main reason she stayed on, despite the lousy pay, were the opportunities she had to meet men. Bunny had said as much.

Before coming to work at Grace Gardens Bunny had been a sales girl at a woman's clothing outlet. "Talk about your wastelands," she had complained. "The only men who go to a woman's clothing store are either married or cross-dressers. She'd related some stories about the latter that had made Austin laugh so hard tears ran down her cheeks.

That was the best thing about Bunny. When she was in a good mood she was irrepressible, bubbly, like a goofy little sister. But when she was in a bad mood . . . well, no one could match that sense of drama. Will didn't stand a chance.

As for Will, he was pretty obvious about his interest in

Bunny. But though they were close to the same age, both in their early twenties, Bunny seemed a little old for Will. He didn't seem to have acquired any social skills where women were concerned. Austin imagined his courtship of Bunny to consist of something like punching her on the arm. She doubted Bunny would appreciate that approach.

"Car coming," Bunny said.

Austin nodded. She too had heard the distinctive sound of tires on gravel as a car pulled into the parking lot. First customer of the day, she thought. But when she looked up, it wasn't a customer walking toward the store.

"Muncie."

He slid open the door and stepped in.

"Hey Sis."

He was her masculine counterpart, four inches taller, fifty pounds heavier, with wide shoulders and narrow hips. They had the same shade of chestnut hair, brown or red depending on the light, the same eyes, as dark as bitter chocolate, and the same lopsided smiles.

She gave him a hug. "About time you got back. Did you drive all night?"

"No, I got in late and went straight home. I was wiped.

"What did you think of the campus?"

"Not bad. Coffee on?"

Austin rolled her eyes, "As usual, I guess I'll have to drag it out of you one piece at a time." She moved down the counter to pour him a cup of coffee, her actions at odds with her tone of mock anger.

"So, you going to Portland State?" Bunny asked.

"Don't know. Pretty expensive," Muncie answered.

"I'd go. I'd do anything to get the hell out of this place.

I'm so sick of snow and slippery streets and having to dig my car out. I hate having to wear ten tons of clothes all the time. If I could get out of here before winter I sure would. I bet I could make a lot more money in Portland and I could meet a lot more interesting people."

Austin made a face at Muncie behind Bunny's back. Like Will, Muncie had also once been interested in Bunny. Austin had been against Muncie dating one of her employees, but he had ignored his sister's concerns and he had gone out with Bunny a few times.

Eventually he realized that Bunny was too immature for him, and he had stopped seeing her. He had confessed that, though he was only a few years older, the whole thing had left him feeling like a lecherous old man. Austin liked to tease him about it whenever she could. She felt it was her duty as his sister to inflict a little character-building pain.

Muncie had come by to make good on his promise to patch hail-blasted holes in the roof of one of the greenhouses.

"Did I tell you how much I appreciate you fixing the roof?" she asked.
"I'm just glad it's only one roof," he replied.
"I'm pretty sure they had the rest of the roofs torn off and replaced. This greenhouse is the smallest and in pretty bad condition. It's definitely got a sort of lean. They probably planned to tear it down."

"Well if it's leaning maybe that's what you should do."

"Oh no, it's leaning against the wind so it should last awhile," she said, joking. "Besides," she added more seriously, "there's no money for new buildings in my budget. I will, however, purchase for you a three-course meal today as a gesture of my thanks. Providing, of course, you don't cost me a fortune by falling through the roof and

33

breaking a leg or something stupid like that."

"Your concern for my safety is touching," Muncie replied. "And the offer of a meal is of course a bonus, unless one of the three courses is French fries?"

"Amazing. Have you always been psychic?"

Muncie shook his head, gathered his tools, took the cup of coffee she offered to him and, without another word, went out through the back door to get started.

Austin went back to work. By nine, the morning mist had burned away and the temperature was steadily climbing. At noon, the sky was a cloudless blue and the temperature a relatively balmy 65 degrees. That was the weather at five thousand feet, completely unpredictable – as unpredictable as the customers. She'd thought such a warm day would get everyone out working on their yards, but only three people came in the entire morning. Things were so quiet that Austin decided she would join Muncie for lunch at a restaurant in town. She couldn't wait to ask him about his time in Portland.

They sat at a booth and their waitress, one of Austin's regulars, came right over. They chatted for a minute about the new hybrid roses and whether they would really be tough enough to withstand a Blue Spruce winter. Then she took Austin and Muncie's order to the kitchen, her white nurses' shoes incongruous with the crisp white blouse and narrow black skirt she wore.

Austin looked across the table at her brother and felt a sudden, overwhelming sense of sadness. She hoped it didn't show. She busied herself, tearing the wrapper off a straw and stirring the glass of ice water in front of her, ice clinking against the glass.

"So," she said brightly. "I guess you'll be heading for the big city soon."

"I'm a big city kind of guy."

"I know you are. I keep thinking you should be designing houses, not building them from someone else's plans."

"I will eventually. It's not like I've been wasting my time. It's good to have a solid background in construction."

"I guess you're right. It's just that I feel like the only reason you moved here was, well, for me."

"Not just for you. I didn't feel any more rooted then you did. Besides, getting away from Debbie was good for me."

"She was toxic."

"Yes, but if we'd stayed in Denver I'd probably be married to her right now. We'd have two point five children, a golden retriever and a minivan."

"There isn't anything wrong with that. That's what a lot of people want, you know."

"With the right person, maybe that's enough, but with Debbie? I don't know."

"No. Not with Debbie. I never could understand the attraction. Of course, I never could see the attraction to Bunny either."

"Really? Strange, and it was right there in front of her the whole time."

"Disgusting." Austin pelted Muncie with a tiny bag of Sweet n' Low. He would have retaliated, but the waitress appeared with their lunch and they were forced to pretend to be grownups.

CHAPTER 5

After lunch they drove back to the store, but even before Muncie had pulled his truck into a parking space they could hear the screaming. Exchanging glances, they hurried in. Bunny and Will were standing face to face, only inches apart, faces distorted with anger, and yelling so loudly that it hurt Austin's ears.

"What the hell is going on in here?" Austin demanded.

"Ask the princess," Will barked.

"Kiss my ass," Bunny snapped back.

"Somebody better tell me what's going on, or both of you are walking out of here."

"If anybody's getting fired it ought to be him. Why don't you ask him about the plants he's growing behind the jade in the little greenhouse?"

"Will, are you growing weed on my property?" Austin asked.

"Uh, I mean. . .well uh yeah, but only a couple of plants. Just for personal use."

"Do I look like a cop to you? I don't care how much or

what for. Do you know I could lose my business, my property? Get out there and get rid of it. Muncie, go with him and make sure he does it."

"Am I fired?" Will asked.

"I don't know. Don't talk to me right now."

"I think that means you're not fired," offered Muncie as he led the way toward the door.

When they were gone Austin said, "Okay, this is your chance. Tell me what this is all about."

Bunny took a tissue from the box on the counter and dabbed her eyes. "Well, it's kind of personal."

"When you bring it to work it's no longer personal," replied Austin curtly.

"I guess," Bunny agreed reluctantly. "Me and Will were sort of seeing each other and he got me pregnant. Well, anyway I thought he did. Turned out I wasn't."

"Oh?"

"Yeah, and then when I told him I was pregnant you know what he said?"

Austin had a pretty good idea, but she just shook her head.

"He asked me who the father was. The jerk. I told him I knew it was his. Then he said he'd get some money from his old man and I could get an abortion. He never even asked if I wanted one or not." Bunny burst into fresh tears. Austin felt at a complete loss as to how to respond. She rubbed her hands across her face. Was she an employer or a babysitter? Sometimes it seemed like the same thing.

"Maybe you'd better go home and get some rest. I can see you're really stressed. I want you to take the rest of the day off."

"I can't. I need the hours."

"Well then, how about you go home for just awhile. Come back late this afternoon and finish planting those bulb pots that Will started this morning."

At mention of his name Bunny wrinkled her nose and looked on the verge of another round of tears. Austin went behind the counter to retrieve Bunny's purse. Handing it to her, Austin hustled her to the door. Go on. Go home. Do I need to drive you?"

Bunny shook her head, took her purse and reached inside for a tissue. She blew her nose, wiped her eyes, looked at her watch, and with a trembling smile said, "I can drive myself."

Austin watched as Bunny, stiff-backed, head held high and hips swaying provocatively, made her way to the far side of the parking lot and got into her little red Jetta.

After a short time Muncie and Will returned to the store and Austin looked up from the inventory sheet she'd been working on.

"Well, what did you find?" she asked, directing her question to Muncie.

"He wasn't lying. It was only two plants. Real nice ones though."

"Did you destroy them?"

"Well, we de-leafed them, chopped them into little pieces and we fully intend to burn them."

Austin cocked one eyebrow and said, "Please, don't tell me more. No, wait–you," she looked at Will. "What the hell were you thinking? Bunny told me what you were fighting about. I know your personal life is not my business, but you keep trying to make it mine."

"It was stupid, I know," Will explained. "We were here

late one night; one thing led to another. . .it was just a one-night-stand. No different than what she's done with just about every– "

"Don't. Don't say it. It takes two and she wasn't alone in this. Just be damn glad she isn't pregnant."

"Oh man, you can believe it," he said.

"What a mess. I just hope you learned something. She's coming back later tonight, to make up some of her hours. So make sure you don't stay late tonight. I don't want you two alone together, at least for a while. Got it?"

"Yes."

"Good," Austin said.

Later that afternoon, right before closing, the phone rang.

"Austin," Bunny said in a hoarse whisper that Austin thought was almost certainly faked, "I'm not feeling very well. I think I'm coming down with something. Do you mind if I don't come in tonight?"

"No, that's all right," Austin said, trying to keep the irritation out of her voice. "Call tomorrow if you aren't going to make it in."

"OK."

So much for needing hours, thought Austin. Unfortunately. both Muncie and Will had gone home. Austin let out the sigh she'd been suppressing. She might as well get out there and get to work. Not like she had anywhere better to be.

She'd chickened out on calling Blake. She'd been hoping her friend Janice would stop by and prod her into it. Then she'd remembered that Janice didn't own a business—she had a life. She may have even spent the day doing something fun, like Christmas shopping.

Thinking about Christmas and what gifts she might buy for the people she cared about, Austin shut down the store, took her coat and keys, and headed out back. The way was well-lit and she was grateful. A frosty wind was blowing, pushing a bank of dark clouds ahead of it. She would finish potting up the bulbs so they'd have plenty of color spots to sell in early spring. She loved those first blooms the most. Crocus blossoms pushing through the snow was one of her favorite sights.

Here she was thinking about spring, and winter was just arriving. It was going to be a cold one, too. According to one of her customers, you could tell because the caterpillars were wearing heavy coats this year. They were clever things, those caterpillars.

Austin lifted out the wooden bar that held the door shut, leaned it against the wall, then stepped inside and pulled the chain that turned on the single bulb hanging from the ceiling. She shut the door behind her, cutting off the chill and blustery wind, tossed her coat on top of a stack of trays, and pulled on a pair of gloves.

The shed was ten feet wide and twelve deep. A heap of Austin's own special mix of potting soil took up most of the space, along with stacked bags of peat moss, perlite and compost.

A waist-high table stood along the back wall, a fist-sized hole in its surface opening to a wheeled recovery bin underneath. Below the table, on both sides of the bin, shelves held an assortment of sterile clay pots. Open bags of crocus, tulips, daffodils, and other spring flowering bulbs sat on the table, along with an assortment of hand trowels, stakes, and tags. Austin bent over, slid a stack of pots off a shelf and put them on the table. Should have a radio in here, she thought idly.

She began to hum to herself and was contentedly filling the pots with soil and arranging the bulbs in artistic patterns when the light went out.

Chapter 6

Darkness.

Austin froze in place. Bulb burned out–that's all. The door is behind you, she reminded herself. There is nothing to be afraid of. You are a big girl and you are not afraid of the dark. Even as she said it she could feel the beginning of panic, the sense of weight pressing down, cutting off her breath. She took a step back, then turned slowly. Holding her hands out in front of her, eyes wide open, but unable to see anything, she took one hesitant step.

Step by careful step, she made her way to the door. Her fingertips touched rough cut lumber. She pushed, and there was enough give to let her know she had found the door and not a wall, but the door did not open. She pushed again. Again the door swayed slightly and then came up hard against some obstruction.

"Hey, is anyone out there?" she called.

Nothing but silence answered her. She found the door latch and shook it hard.

"Hello?"

Again there was no answer, and no light, not even from under the door. What had happened to the yard lights? Why wouldn't the door open? She hit the door with her fists. She screamed, the eerie sound echoing around her, pushing her fear to an even higher level. She tried to scream again but found she didn't have enough air. A weight was pressing down on her chest, constricting her lungs so she couldn't fill them. She hammered on the door.

Then, between the echoes of her pounding fists she thought—yes she could hear it, something was in here—something—she gasped for air. She felt dizzy. Red and yellow sparks of light swam in front of her eyes. She began to sway and then she was falling, not in a graceful swoon, but in a dead faint, crashing hard onto the wooden floor.

She woke to the feeling of someone's hands on her upper arms, fingers tight enough to bruise. Her eyes flew open. Light. The world swam dizzily for a moment and then settled and the face above her, a confusion of dark and light angles, resolved itself.

"Muncie?"

"Are you OK?"

"I was locked in. It was dark." She could hear herself practically blubbering but she couldn't stop herself. It didn't matter. To Muncie, what she'd said was explanation enough.

He had pulled her out of the shed and into the yard and there was light, light from the yard lights, light from the shed. He was kneeling beside her. Gently he pulled her into a sitting position and wrapped his arms around her shoulders. She started crying.

"Shhh. It's OK."

"This wasn't some stupid joke, was it? You weren't pulling a prank? No, never mind. Of course not, you wouldn't do that." Austin corrected herself.

"But someone sure as hell did," Muncie said. Think about it, Austin. Who would do this to you?"

"I don't know," Austin said, shaking her head.

"Well I'm sure as hell going to find out. For now though let's just get you home. I think your elbow's bleeding." As soon as he mentioned it, Austin felt a stinging in her elbow.

"It feels like I skinned it. Or maybe I scratched it on a nail. Oh Muncie, I am so sick of this. Do you think I'll ever outgrow it?"
Muncie didn't answer. Austin got to her feet and found a new ache, this time in her hip.

"Are you all right?"

"I think so."

"I'd better follow you home."

"You don't have– "

"I'm going to follow you home. You wouldn't be like this. . . "

"Don't," Austin insisted. "Don't talk like that. Just follow me home. I'll be grateful if you'd do that."

Muncie nodded and said nothing more.

Chapter 7

Saturday dawned bright and cold, and business was brisk. Austin couldn't keep the nursery open seven days a week, so had opted to close on Sundays and Mondays. That way, customers with "normal" weekends off could come in on Saturday and on Monday she could do her banking and other errands. Of course it was rare that she actually took the days off. Most Mondays found her trying to catch up or finish some project.

Paco and Justin stopped by the nursery several times throughout the day to pick up loads of bark and decorative rock for their lawn care customers. To Austin it seemed like everyone in town was a little frantic, all aware that the first big snow could hit at any time. Or maybe what she was sensing wasn't their agitation but a leftover from her panic attack.

Refusing to dwell on the incident, Austin shifted her thoughts to a more current issue. She was determined to keep everyone off the unemployment rolls as long as she could.

"How would you feel about operating a snow plow?"

45

she had asked Paco back in August. He had liked the idea.

"Last winter the county hired me to haul snow from the streets," he said. "They have not enough people for this job. They have a crane that picks up the snow and puts it in the truck, then I drive to the river and shovel it out. I made many trips. If the winter is bad and the county cannot keep up with the snow this year, maybe they will hire us. Maybe the big businesses will hire us too. They need their parking lots open so the customers will come."

"That's what I was thinking," Austin said, growing more enthusiastic about the idea. "Some days we can do residential driveways, and other days commercial parking lots. Maybe we won't get rich, but at least I won't have to keep stretching nine or ten months of work to cover 12 months of bills."

Just as she was replaying that conversation, Paco walked in. Austin reminded him of the snowplow idea and asked if he still thought she should go ahead.

"A wonderful idea," he enthused.

"That's it then. Monday I'll talk to the bank about a loan for the plow."

"Well, only if you are not too busy with the other things."

"What other things?"

"That man, he come looking for you. Saw the truck and asked for where you are. You are going to have dinner with him soon, I think."

"Ha, you think so, do you?"

"Yes, it is known how you like the cowboys."

"Paco, I am so sorry, but that has cost you another raise."

"Ha ha, you are making me to laugh. A raise. Ha ha."

When Austin got home that evening, she didn't even take off her jacket before picking up the phone. She had spent the entire drive home talking herself into making the call. She wasn't going to take the chance she'd change her mind if she stopped her momentum. She dialed the number she'd scribbled on the cover of her phone book earlier.

"Hi, this is Blake," she heard, as his voice mail system picked up. She almost hung up, but the message was short and she was caught by the beep. She had to talk now, or leave one of those awful dead air messages and her phone number trapped in his caller ID.

"Hi, It's Austin," she mumbled. "I was just. . .

There was a screech in her ear and then his voice.

"Austin. Sorry. I was just walking in the door and heard your voice."

"Oh," she mumbled. "I was just . . . well I . . ."

"I've been out looking at property for two straight days," he said, rescuing her. That real estate woman must have dragged me to every corner of the valley, and around back of every mountain. For such a small town this sure is a big area."

"That's true," agreed Austin. "The town may be small, but the county is huge."

"Well it's making the options a lot tougher than I expected, and my need for some good advice even more important. I sure would appreciate it if I could get some of that advice from you. I'd be willing to pay with dinner? Tomorrow?"

"Tomorrow, or Monday if that would be better."

"Tomorrow is great. How about you meet me at that steak house on Main Street."

47

"Sam's Grill?" she asked.

"Yes, that's the one. What time?"

"Oh, I don't care. Six too late?"

"Perfect. I'll see you there at six."

"Fine."

Austin hung up and took a deep breath. She hadn't been on a date in several months. Well, it was done now so no use worrying about it, at least until Sunday. Sunday! Oh no. She suddenly remembered that she had promised Janice they'd go canoeing on Sunday. Janice had been bugging her to get one last trip down Broken River in before snowfall.

Well, maybe if Janice agreed to get an early start she could fit both in, she reasoned. Days off were too rare to waste and besides, if she stayed home all day she'd be a total wreck by dinner time.

Shrugging out of her jacket, Austin picked up the phone again. Not only would Janice understand about leaving early, she was certain she could count on Janice to keep her from changing her mind about meeting Blake for dinner, a thought that had crossed her mind half a dozen times in the last five minutes alone.

On Sunday morning Austin got up and dressed in waterproof boots, jeans, a sheepskin lined jacket and a bright orange hunter's cap. The county was home to a great many hunters who, if they weren't hunting, were practicing. Janice had taught her that it was a good idea to not look too much like wildlife.

At the sound of her friend's car pulling into the driveway, Austin hurried out. The canoe was tied to the roof of Janice's compact. Austin had to smile at how strange it looked, prow and stern hanging far past the front and rear bumpers.

Austin tossed her backpack into the back seat and slid into the passenger seat, eager to bring Janice up to date on her phone call with Blake. Janice, a diminutive, natural red head with a sprinkling of freckles and flashing green eyes gave Austin a wide smile.

"Well, are you ready to shoot the rapids?" she asked.

"I'm ready to paddle gently across a mirror-still pond if that's what you're asking," Austin answered

"Exactly what I meant."

"Good."

"However, you're not getting off so easy on this guy. I want to hear all about him, and I want it in graphic detail," demanded Janice.

"We haven't even gone out yet. How much graphic detail could there be?"

"I packed beer and, in case it's real nasty, a pint of brandy. Somewhere in there we should be able to find some kind of detail, even if we have to invent it."

Austin agreed, as she usually did, with Janice's innate wisdom.

Chapter 8

It took Austin no more than an hour to prepare for her date. Considering she'd returned from her canoe trip with blistered hands, wind-burned skin, and a slight beer buzz, she thought she was doing pretty well.

By the time she climbed into her pickup she had changed into white jeans, a black turtleneck, and dangerously high-heeled black boots. She left her hair down for a change, brushing it until it gleamed like burnished mahogany, and instead of the usual minimal eyeliner and lip gloss, she had gone the whole way by smoothing on foundation, and adding blush and eye shadow to her routine.

She had to admit she didn't look half bad. A few drops of her favorite cologne and she was ready.

She continued to feel good about herself, and about the date, until she reached the restaurant. Seeing the cars in the parking lot, knowing people would see her out with Blake, made her incredibly self-conscious. Her stomach fluttered as she climbed out of the truck and slid the keys into her slender black purse. This is silly, she told herself.

Then she took a deep, wavering breath, squared her shoulders and walked into the restaurant.

Blake was already there, waiting for her. That was nice. It would have been harder to sit and wait, the fear that he might not show up, gnawing at her self-esteem.

He looked good, she thought. He stood to pull out her chair. She realized she was doing a precarious emotional balancing act. She was torn between being ridiculously close to bolting for the door and safety, or forgetting dinner entirely and inviting him to her house for the night; which would at least provide some of those details Janet was so eager to hear about.

The waiter helped her past the awkward moment by asking what they'd like to drink. She turned her attention gratefully to the wine list, embarrassed at how quickly her mind had taken her and Blake to her house, her bedroom, her bed. It had been a long time since she'd invited anyone into her bed. She'd almost decided she was fine with the way things were: celibate, but too busy to dwell on the fact. Now she realized how lonely she'd been, an almost desperate loneliness. That bothered her. There was nothing attractive or sexy about desperation. A sure way to ruin a relationship was to act as needy as she suddenly felt.

She ordered a glass of white wine and forced herself to appear relaxed and confident. It was a fine bit of acting, and she thought she was carrying it off well.

Blake began the conversation by asking about different parts of the county. Did she know of any problems with water? Austin found it was easy to slip into her business side, where she spent most of her time, and out of her romantic side, where she was basically a stranger.

Talk of growing seasons and planting led to talking about the nursery and the landscaping business, but as the evening went on, and the lights dimmed, the conversation shifted. It was subtle at first, talk about work and then about goals and values. Soon they were deep in discussion about their shared hope of owning land, staying in one place, putting down roots. He spoke of his wish for a large family, of children and grandchildren who would stay and work the same land. She talked about moving too much as a child and wanting a real home, a place worth defending.

By the end of the evening she had decided it would be easy to fall in love with him. She didn't realize how late it had become until she heard a waiter clear his throat and looked up to notice they were the last customers in the restaurant. Embarrassed, she reached for her purse and her credit card. Blake's hand closed around hers.

"Please, let me get this. I asked you to come for selfish reasons, to ask you about the valley. You've more than earned your supper."

"Don't be silly. If you pay it will feel like a date."

"Great. Then I'm definitely paying."

There was little argument she could make to that. She let him hand the waiter his money with no further protest.

Afterwards he walked her to her pickup in the parking lot. Their two vehicles, and a line of employees' cars at the back of the lot, were the only ones there. Again, Austin was aware of how much time had passed, and how easily.

When they reached her truck Austin unlocked the door and Blake reached around her, his arm just brushing hers, and opened it for her. She climbed inside, then turned slightly to say goodnight. For a moment she thought he was going to reach into the truck and put his arm around her. For a moment she considered whether she should lean forward and let him kiss her. Then the moment passed. He closed the door and she rolled down the window.

"Can we do this again soon?" he asked.

"I think that would be fine," she replied. "Call me."

"Oh, I will. You can count on that."

Austin smiled.

"Now you better get home. You look sleepy, and I don't want you falling asleep on that windy road."

"Oh, that's not a problem," she joked, "I can drive it in my sleep. I've done it plenty of times."

"I'm sure you can. But just to humor me, how about you stay awake just until you reach your driveway?"

Austin agreed, and he stepped back and waved as she rolled up her window.

Cold was settling in, a wispy mist curling around the tires of the pickup and a fine film of ice beginning to coat the windshield. Austin turned the truck on and cranked up the heat. Her knees felt half frozen, but at least in a few moments she'd be able to see the road.

She made it home safely, though her frequent yawning reminded her that she was, by nature, a morning person. This staying up all hours of the night was not something she was used to. She wasn't a kid anymore, she reminded herself. She had responsibilities, a business to run, a house to manage.

Despite all that, she hoped Blake would call and they could do it all again soon, just as he'd asked. Too tired to do more than brush her teeth and get undressed, she crawled into bed and was asleep in moments.

Chapter 9

In the early hours of morning she woke, as dazed and disoriented as if she had been drugged. She fought through the lassitude with difficulty, trying to understand what could have pulled her from such a deep and lovely sleep.

She lay quietly for awhile, listening, straining for some sound, but all she heard was the intermittent ticking of the furnace as it cooled down between cycles. She stretched and thought about what it would be like to be waking up with Blake beside her.

Then she opened her eyes—to darkness.

The darkness was absolute, the kind that makes you wonder if your eyes are open. She reached up and touched her eyes and a feeling of déjà vu swept through her.

"No," she said out loud. She would not let this happen. But despite her wishes, fear, a pulsing wave, drew around her, constricting her chest until she was gasping for air, her heart racing, the sound hammering in her ears. She fought with the fear, tried to reason with it. Electrical outage, that's all. The lights are out because of a power failure. Nothing strange there. Happens all the time. Wind in the wires. She took a deep breath and rolled out of bed and to her feet.

Flashlight. In the table beside the bed. She fumbled for the drawer pull, felt for the cold weight of the flashlight, for a moment just knowing the flashlight was there, heavy in her hand, seemed to make the darkness recede. She put her thumb on the switch, slid it forward.

Nothing happened. She shook the flashlight thinking, maybe a loose bulb, a bad connection. She always checked the damn thing. Had she forgotten. She slid the switch back and forth several times, shook it again. Nothing.

She let the flashlight fall back into the drawer with a thump. The dark was deeper now, like some malignant force. She could almost sense it laughing at her idiotic stumbling, at her forgetfulness. Then she remembered.

Matches—candles in the living room. She took a step toward where the door should be. Her legs felt weak and wobbly, but then sheer terror strengthened them, and she lunged for the doorway—the way out. Misjudging the distance in the dark and in her haste, she slammed face first into the edge of the door. She rebounded backward, her foot coming down on one of the high heeled boots she'd dropped on the floor before falling into bed. Losing her balance, arms pinwheeling, she fell backward. The back of her head slammed into the hard brass footboard of her bed. She slid sideways to the floor, coming to rest on her side, her left arm twisted behind her.

When she regained consciousness, she opened her eyes. Darkness. She tried to get to her feet. Her arm was numb, but as she rolled to her knees her hand began to tingle, and she realized it had only fallen asleep. She had been laying on it. She didn't know for how long. The back of her head hurt, and her eye throbbed and ached. None of that mattered as much as the darkness.

Cursing her weakness, she got to her feet and stepped carefully forward, feeling ahead until she found the bedroom door. It was closed. She opened it. Candles. Matches. If she could get to them quickly, before the panic overcame her sense of reason. As she stepped through the doorway into the hallway, the hallway light inexplicably came on.

She always kept that light on and her bedroom door open enough so that the light kept the shadows back in the corners where they belonged. In every other room of her house a night-light winked on and from down the hallway she heard a low thump as the furnace started up.

"Son of a bitch," she cursed. She hurried straight into the living room anyway, took a book of matches from a basket on the mantle and slipped them in the shirt pocket of her pajamas before stumbling to the bathroom to view the damage.

Her right eye ached and the skin around it felt hot. She squinted at the mirror. The eye itself seemed fine, but there was a dark red line running vertically above and below it through her eyebrow and across her cheek. The skin around the line was puffy and mottled, but the skin was not broken.

Muttering to herself, she went into the kitchen and pulled a bag of frozen peas out of the freezer. Turning from the freezer, she looked through the kitchen window and saw that the sun would be rising soon. Already there was a line of light gray mist on the horizon, the line highlighting the crest of the mountains, the shadows of pine trees, as jagged as a serrated knife.

She sat at the kitchen table and gingerly placed the cold

bag of peas against her eye, and then, for no reason she could explain, she began to laugh. She didn't know why she found it so funny, sitting at the kitchen table at four in the morning with a cold bag of peas pressed against her face. She did know that every time she laughed her eye throbbed, but that only made her laugh harder.

Chapter 10

On Monday morning, Austin was reaching for the phone to call Janice when it rang. She wasn't at all surprised to find Janice on the other end. That sort of coincidence was normal for them. From the first day they'd met as juniors in college, the two had clicked. Sometimes it was as if they shared the same mind. It wasn't only that they agreed on most of the big issues, such as ethics, politics, and religion, but that they processed information and dealt with emotions in very similar ways.

Although alike in many of the ways that mattered, they didn't look at all alike. Austin was tall and dark, with an obviously Northern European ancestry, while petite Janice, with her green eyes and curly light red hair, was so stereotypically Irish she looked like she had walked out of a travel brochure for the Emerald Isle.

"Hey, I was about to call you."

"Of course you were. I don't have classes today." Janice taught first grade at Alice Hall elementary. "Want to meet at the Dolphin for lunch, say noon?"

"You're on."

Austin arrived first and slid into a red vinyl-covered booth in the corner. A few minutes later, Janice showed up. The first thing she said was, "My God, Austin, what happened to you?"

"I know, I know. I feel really stupid. I don't even want to talk about it."
"Well, you're going to."

"It was nothing, really. The lights went out last night, and I woke up and, well, you know I have these little anxiety attacks. I sort of stumbled around and ran into a doorway. Yes, I know it's sort of a cliché and maybe hard to believe, but that's really the way it happened."

"Are you kidding? I totally believe you. I know what a klutz you are. Remember graduation day, when we decided to put dye in the fountain and you fell in?"

"How could I forget? I was the only Smurf to receive a bachelor's degree that year."

"It wasn't that bad; just your hands. And I thought you looked very "Grace Kelly" with the white gloves."

Austin groaned at the memory.

"Anyway, back to the real issue here. This panic attack."

"It wasn't a panic attack."

"Anxiety attack, then. Is that better?"

Austin began to fuss with the small arrangement of blue silk flowers in the cheap plastic vase on the table. "Well, more like a mild anxiety attack, but okay. So I was thinking, maybe you're right, maybe it is time I talk to someone. I was wondering. Do you still have the number of that shrink you told me about?"
"Licensed Professional Counselor," Janice corrected her friend. "Sure, I've got it. His name is Mark Harworth," she

said, reaching for her purse. "Half the women teachers at school are seeing him. I think they're making up mental health conditions."

"You think he's still taking patients?"

"Probably. His office is pretty new. I haven't talked to him in awhile, though. A few months ago he helped me find some resources for a family, but I haven't needed him since." She found his card and handed it to Austin, who slipped it into the back pocket of her jeans.

Just then the waitress appeared to take their order.

They had their usual, soup and salad with ice water for Janice, cheeseburger, fries and 7-Up for Austin. She always felt a little guilty that her metabolism ran in high gear, while it seemed like Janice couldn't even look at a cookie without gaining a pound.

"So, Janice asked, "You going to tell me about Blake or do I have to drag it out of you crumb by tasty crumb?"

Austin smiled.

"Hmmm, that good?"

"Pretty good." Austin agreed and she told Janice how easy it had been to talk to Blake. "It was almost weird how well we got along. I mean, he seems to want exactly what I want. He even wants the same number of kids, the same kind of lifestyle."

"You find a guy you really like and you call it weird?"

"Well, weird isn't right, I guess. It's just I've never met anyone who seemed so perfect. You know how it is. If they look good, they probably have a wife."

"Or a boyfriend," Janice added.

"Yeah, or a boyfriend. Or they tell you they want the same things you want, but then they don't bother asking what that is."

"Or they mimic what you say, and six months down the road you find out they just played mirror so they could get in your pants."

Austin nodded. "It was different with Blake, though. He told me what he was looking for first, and it was like I was the mirror, or sort of like his echo."

"That sounds awesome."

"And scary."

"So, is he the real reason you wanted Mark's number?"

"Maybe. I guess. Who wants to go out with someone who's afraid of the dark?"

Janice nodded and asked, "So now what? When do you see him again?"

"I don't know. I guess it's up to him. "

"Well, that's a lame answer. Since when did you become shy and demure?"

Austin refused to take the bait and said, "I don't want to chase him. I guess I don't want him to think I'm easy."

"But you *are* easy," her friend joked.

"Oh–that's right. It's been so long I'd forgotten."

Their lunch arrived. The waitress put their plates and drinks in front of them and asked if they had everything they needed. Austin told her they were fine. As she walked away, Austin asked Janice, "Is today the day?"

"I don't think so," said Janet. "You ask."

"No way."

"So what you're saying is we will never know."

"Probably not," Janice agreed.

The Blue Dolphin was a converted Airstream trailer.

To the left of the entrance stood a towering, thirty-foot tall blue neon dolphin that would have looked more at home tacked to the front of a Vegas casino.

Austin's theory was that the cranky owner had made a good deal on it. Janice held the more romantic notion that the owner was once involved with a man whose memory was tied to dolphins. Maybe the man had a dolphin tattoo, maybe he died deep-sea fishing. Her theories were many, and varied from improbable to impossible. Austin had so much fun hearing them that she didn't really want to know the truth. It was a small-town pastime, but Spruce was a small town.

As soon as Austin left the restaurant, she swung by the nursery to see if a delivery she'd been expecting had arrived. It hadn't. She decided she might as well make some phone calls.

First she called Bunny to see how she was feeling and to learn if she planned to work the next morning. An answering machine picked up. Three separate voices, including Bunny's, identified themselves and then all together they chanted, "Sorry we're not in right now, we hate to make you wait, but if you'd called at the right time, that wouldn't be your fate." This was followed by a chorus of giggles. Austin rolled her eyes and waited for the tone so she could leave a message, instead there was a click and a woman's voice said,

"Hello?"

"Hello. Bunny?"

"No. This is her roommate, Zoe."

"Oh, sorry. Do you know when Bunny will be in?" Austin asked.

"No. She didn't come home last night, but she does

that a lot. She'll probably show up today sometime. Or not."

"I see. Well, if you see her will you tell her to call Grace Gardens?"

"Oh, sure. No problem. She'll probably be home real soon."

"Ok. Thank you."

Trying to decide at what level of annoyed she wanted to be, Austin fished the counselor's business card Janice had given her out of her pocket.

She was surprised when Mark Harworth himself answered the phone, even more surprised when he said, "I've had a cancellation this afternoon, so if you can get here in an hour I'd be happy to see you today."

Caught without an excuse, Austin took the appointment. When she hung up, she realized she would have very little time to spend on worrying about seeing this therapist. Maybe that was for the best. Spilling her life story to a stranger always seemed like such an invasion of her privacy and so potentially embarrassing, like walking down Main Street in your underwear–by choice.

She spent a few moments rearranging shelves that were perfectly fine. Then she used the mirror in the tiny bathroom to brush her hair and reapply her eyeliner. Looking at her watch she realized it was already time to go. Gathering her jacket, gloves and courage, she locked the store and climbed into her truck.

As she drove, Austin tried to imagine how the appointment would go. From his voice on the phone, and her past experience with therapists, she thought she could construct a pretty clear picture of him. He would be in his late forties with gray hair and a neatly clipped beard. He'd wear a nice suit, a tie, and polished shoes, probably black or dark brown. He'd have a bit of a paunch and effeminate hands.

She imagined his office would be lined with dark paneling and hold a big leather couch, some oversized chairs and a mahogany desk, which he would sit behind authoritatively. And of course there would be a tall bookcase full of books with titles like *Behavior Modification: Methods Of*, or *Sexual Deviance: Pros and Cons*. She smiled at her twisted imagination.

Eventually, she'd tell him about her phobias, and he'd tell her she needed the latest anti-anxiety medication. She'd fill the prescription, come home, flush the pills down the toilet and get on with it. She didn't have time for this. It was going to cost a small fortune, too. She should turn around and get back to work. Of course, he'd probably make her pay for the appointment anyway. She sighed; might as well get her money's worth.

She pulled into the parking lot of the old downtown Medical Center, a three-story stucco building that had been the area's only hospital until the new one was built three years ago. Townspeople still called it the Medical Center, though it now housed offices for dentists, a chiropractor, a private investigator, two different insurance companies, and a therapist.

She ignored the elevator and took the carpeted stairs. The stairwell smelled of paint and carpet glue with an undercurrent of mold. It was as if the building was saying no matter how much sky blue paint you splash around, or how much beige carpeting you install, I am still undeniably old.

The entrance to Suite 301 was one of a half dozen doors, spaced equally along the third floor hallway. Each was different from the next, only because of the discreet brass numbers hung at eye level. For a moment she hesitated, wondering if she should knock or just walk in. It's an office, she decided, they expect you to walk in. She turned the knob and stepped into what turned out to be a small waiting area. There was no receptionist, only a short counter to her left with a sign that read, *Please take a seat. We will be with you shortly.*

Austin took a seat in one of the two mission-style leather chairs against the wall on the right. There was a door set in the far wall that she assumed led to an office. She wondered how he would know she was there. She looked around trying to get a feel for his personality.

The chairs were tasteful reproductions, burgundy leather and cherry-toned wood. Between them, a slate-topped table held a lamp with a heavy iron base and a fan of magazines. She read their titles: *Good Housekeeping, People, National Geographic, Newsweek.* No help there.

There was only one picture on the walls, right above the counter. Austin stood up to get a better look at it. Framed in the same cherry-stained wood as the chairs was a painting of a futuristic city, but as she stared at it, she realized something was wrong. There were fish swimming through the windows and across the sky. Seaweed, not vines, growing around the columns. Everything was underwater. It seemed obvious to her now, but at first it was as if her mind had refused to see what it didn't expect. Well, if that wasn't a great advertisement for the faultiness of perception. But it still didn't tell her much about the man who, she conjectured, had hung it there.

She heard the click of a doorknob and turned.

"It's a Nogeth. Do you like it?"

"I do. It makes you wonder if what you see is really

there, and wonder what might still be there that you don't see."

"Exactly. You must be Austin Ward. I'm Mark Harworth," he said. "You can call me Mark. Sorry if I kept you," He stepped across the room with his hand extended. "I was on the phone."

"That's okay, I wasn't waiting long."

She preceded him into the office. It was well-lit by a row of windows that looked out over the parking lot. There was a long couch under the window and a couple of mismatched leather recliners, one brown one black, facing it. Between the chairs was a table and the usual box of Kleenex.

"Please sit down, anywhere you like," the therapist said.

Austin chose the brown chair. As she sat down she took a quick look around, comparing her imagination with reality, she decided she'd been about fifty percent right.

The couch under the windows was also covered in leather, like the chairs, but so old its entire surface was covered with a fine cobweb of cracks. It looked too comfortable to sit on. She thought it would be the perfect couch for a therapist, the kind that would lure you in and make you want to lie down, and once you were there, and helplessly comfortable, it would draw out all your darkest, most private thoughts.

The walls were paneled and had probably been some dark imitation wood grain but were now painted eggshell white. There was a big desk, but he couldn't sit behind it and still talk to a client. It was shoved against the wall and to sit at it he'd have to have his back to her. Its surface held a computer, a printer, a fax machine, a phone, and a stacking file almost buried under folders. The wall above the desk had become a bulletin board, and layers of brochures and documents had been thumbtacked all over it.

The bookcase she'd expected was also present and reached from floor to ceiling, taking up the entire wall opposite the desk. As large as it was, it sagged under the massive weight of books and professional journals, but she also noted several stacks of paperbacks and magazines. At a quick glance the paperbacks were by King, Sandford, and Mitchner and the magazines were *Northwest Paddler* and *Cross Country Skier*. So, he was a man who read for entertainment, and liked outdoor activities. It was a good start.

She slid back farther into the chair. Mark sat down in the black chair that was beside hers but angled so that they could look at each other comfortably. She decided that while she had been fifty-percent right about his office, she had been one-hundred percent wrong about him.

He couldn't have been more than thirty, thirty-five tops. Instead of gray, his hair was dark brown, thick and wavy, and long enough to reach his collar. There was no beard or mustache. Instead of a suit he wore khaki Dockers, a pale blue Oxford shirt that set off a dark tan, and hiking boots. He was a couple inches taller than Austin, five-ten or eleven, and heavy without being fat. He looked like an ex-football or wrestling jock, not at all like her vision of an aging Freud wannabe.

"Where'd you get your name?" he asked. "It's very unusual."

"Yes, and usually a boy's name, I guess. My mom thought it up. My dad was in the army and we moved a lot, so my mom decided it would be fun to name her kids after the places we were conceived.

"That could have been tragic."

"Tell my brother," she said, "Muncie."

"Ouch."

"Yeah, but the ironic thing is that Dad was never stationed where we were conceived. They were there because they were on vacation or visiting friends or something."

"Do your parents live in town?"

Austin shook her head. "No, my mom died four years ago, in Colorado. Cancer. They had retired there. My dad died about nine months later."

"Janice told me she'd given you my card and you might be calling. She mentioned to me that you'd bought the old nursery on Spring Hill road."

"Yes, just a few months ago. When my father died he left me a small inheritance. It was enough to buy the house I'd been renting and the nursery. Now all I have to do is come up with enough to keep them both from falling apart. The house and the business are both fixer-uppers with a lot of fixing up to do."

"Sounds like that could get pretty stressful. Is that the reason you've come to see me today?"

The question reminded Austin of where she was. If getting someone to talk was the sign of a good therapist, then Mark must be a good one. She couldn't believe how easy she found it to discuss things. Well, at least the surface things–her parents and her business; but to talk about the rest? To really look at the bad places and the emotions that came with them. She wasn't so sure she could do that.

"You've got a nice black eye there," he said, covering the awkward silence that had greeted his question. "Run into a door, did you?"

Austin burst into laughter, and Mark smiled with her, without knowing why.

Somehow the laughter made it easier for her to admit the reason she had come. She blurted it out in a rush. "I'm twenty-six years old and I'm so afraid of the dark that if the lights go out, yes, I panic and run into doors. It's silly and embarrassing, and I doubt you can do anything about it, but that's the problem. Well, that and the other thing."

"Other thing?"

"Well, I'm not only afraid of the dark. I'm also afraid of closed spaces—offices without windows, elevators, mummy sleeping bags. Sometimes even going through a carwash can sort of freak me out. Well, to be totally honest, the only time I ever went through a carwash I freaked out, and I have never used one since. I avoid situations like that. I guess that's why I went into landscaping. You get to be outside most of the time. Well, unless someone locks you in a potting shed."

Mark was curious, so she explained about being locked in the shed and finished by telling him the conclusion she and Muncie had come to.

"You see, Will knew Bunny was going to be working there that night. He must have decided it would be a good way to pay her back for telling me about the marijuana plants. I don't think he realized I was the one in the shed. It was a mean prank, but I don't think he meant to hurt anyone. All he did was slip the bar across the door and switch the power off at the electrical box. The box is up by the store so he probably never heard me yell or, if he did, he thought I was Bunny and deserved it."

"And you didn't fire him?"

"I know. Most people probably would have. I just think that now that he knows it was me who got trapped in the potting shed, he must be embarrassed and realize what a stupid idea it was. Maybe he's grown up a little. He's great with plants." She added, lamely, "A real green thumb." Then she realized that once again she was defending a decision she'd made. It made her angry that she had to justify every step, and even angrier when she realized no one was asking her to justify her actions except herself.

"Let's review what you've told me," Mark said. He took a legal pad and pen from the table between the two chairs and scribbled as he spoke. "You live here in town and own a landscaping business as well as a nursery. You employ four people, who frankly sound a little nutso, to use a professional term. You have been suffering from a fear of the dark and of closed spaces for . . . how long would you say?"

"Since I was seven, I guess."

"Interesting. What happened when you were seven?"

"You'll think this is strange, but when I was seven we, my brother and I, were playing in the basement of our apartment building and I got locked inside an old bomb shelter. It must have been pretty scary, and I've been afraid of the dark and being locked in since then."

"Bomb shelter? Well you're right, that is a bit strange."

"Army brats have interesting experiences, I guess. Were your people military?" Austin asked.

"No. Teachers. Dad taught history and Mom taught math."

"Here in Spruce?"

"No, Seattle," he said. "They still live there. They love it, but I was sick of the rain. I much prefer blue skies and snow."

"Then you're in the right place," said Austin.

"I know. It's great. Well, I wish we had more time."
He scribbled a few more words on the pad. "Let's start off
there next time. That is, I'm assuming you want to schedule
another appointment?"

"That would be fine."

"Good. I have some forms I need you to fill out. You
can return them next time."

"All right," Austin said rather stiffly. For a while she'd
forgotten that listening was this man's business. He got
paid to seem interested.

He set the pad down and they both stood. There was a
brief buzzing sound, and he looked toward the door.
Austin realized the sound must be an alarm, alerting him
that someone had come through the front door and into
the reception area.

"Here, let me get you those forms. He went to his desk
and pawed through the piled folders, obviously his idea of a
filing system, until he found the form he wanted. He set
another appointment for the same day and time the
following week, then walked her to the door. She saw that
an attractive woman was sitting in the waiting room and felt
two unmistakable emotions. First, a sense of jealousy and
second, a sense of embarrassment. Immediately she realized
that jealousy was silly. As for the embarrassment of being
seen in his office, well, the woman in the waiting room
probably felt exactly the same way.

Driving toward home, Austin realized how tense she
was. She was gripping the steering wheel and hunched
forward as if preparing to take flight. Other than stopping
for a pack of cigarettes, which she was not about to do,
there was only one other cure she could think of. She drove
past her home, then past Josh's house and up into the hills.
As she drove farther from town, the number of houses and

their welcoming porch lights grew more and more scarce. Finally, all she could see was a luminous full moon, and in the sweep of her headlights, the jagged outline of the trees that lined the road.

She kept catching a flicker, an almost presence, tracking her through the trees. She felt a moment's keen fear, until she realized it was just a ghost cast by one of her own headlights. Her logical mind told her she'd have to remember to have them realigned, while her more primitive side shivered at the thought of ghosts following her in the dark.

She turned up the radio and rolled down the window, breathing deeply of the pine-scented air, the chill wind stroking the side of her face with icy but seductively gentle fingers. Soon the land to her left began to rise.

The ridge which gave the town its name, appeared beside her. Its row of stately blue spruce, planted by someone whose name had been lost, marched in an unnaturally straight line until the road began to curve away and drop down to a wide, slow stretch of the Broken River.

She pulled off the main road into the wide gravel parking area, and right up to the boat ramp, her headlights throwing reflections on the ripples of water. The area was wide enough, open enough, so that she could see by moonlight. In fact, someone had coined the name Moon Meadow for this spot on the river. There was nothing to cast shadows here, and unless it was an unusually cloudy night, no real darkness. Tonight it was clear and the moon was joined by an uncountable number of stars. If the price of that clarity was a fall in temperature, Austin was happy to pay it. This was what she thought of as "her place." The place she came to think and be alone.

Getting out of the truck she walked toward the dock. She passed the haphazardly-placed picnic benches, whose tracery of graffiti, gouged deeply into the wood, shone silver in the moonlight.

She continued alongside the narrow strip of vegetation growing along the waterfront. This was where fishermen drove forked branches into the ground to hold their poles, freeing their hands to bait their children's hooks, or open another beer. She noted the dark rings of soot left on the ground by the tires the night fisherman burned to attract cat fish.

"Light 'tracts them," an old black man had explained one night, when she had been brave enough, or cold enough, to warm herself by his tires' pungent flames.

Afterwards they had become sometime companions, nodding to each other as she made her way to the dock and he slowly rowed his plywood drift boat along the edge of the river. They were content not to speak, but she liked to think they enjoyed each other's silent presence.

As she walked onto the dock it shifted and groaned beneath her feet, little waves formed by the motion moving away to eventually lap at the shore. A breeze came from across the river, bringing a strange but not unpleasant combination of scents; dried hay, fish and snow.

She sat down, making sure the bottom of her coat was between her and the icy planks. Pulling her hat over her ears and her arms into her sleeves she let herself slide into the peacefulness of the water, with its millions of tiny sparks of light.

A glittering bar of light, cast by the moon, seemed to reach across the river. She imagined it to be a fairy path that she could follow and let herself imagine what she might find at the end.

Never once did she consider that her posture, her position in relation to the water, was almost exactly as Granny Birdie had described in her dream.

Chapter 11

On Tuesday, Austin was not surprised that she had to open the store by herself. By the time she had set up the displays, watered the hanging plants and turned the open/closed sign around, she knew that Bunny wasn't going to make an appearance.

Will came in a little late, as usual, but since he often stayed late she didn't comment. She didn't mention Bunny's absence either, and neither did he. They seemed to have come to an unspoken agreement to stay away from that particular subject. They were slammed with customers that morning, and Will stayed inside, helping her wait on them.

In between customers, they discussed the Christmas tree lot. Austin had agreed to rent space to a tree seller who had been asked to move from his usual spot. It was a sure sign that Spruce was growing. Land use ordinances, zones, and restrictions were being more frequently applied and enforced.

"I think we should put in our own trees," Will said. "We've got that hedgerow at the back of the property that isn't doing anything and we could also put them all around the perimeter. Except for the parking lot, of course."

"It's an idea. Let's look into it some more. I'll get on the Net sometime this week and see what I can find."

Will looked up. "Isn't that your friend, the schoolteacher?" Austin turned from the shelf she'd been straightening to see Janice walk in.

"Hi. What are you doing out on a work day?"

"I'm on a break." Janice explained. "I decided to come by to get some poinsettias for the house. I'm going to decorate this year—lights and everything. Then I'm going to invite everyone I know to a Christmas party. Whoever comes, comes. Whoever doesn't gets put on the list."

"Oh really? What list?"

"The list I give to my students. Potential customers for the annual spring seed and cookie sales."

"Ooooh, scary. Say no more, I'll be there," Austin promised.

"I knew I could count on you."

"Things are slowing down up here," interrupted Will. I'm going to get started out back."

"Okay, thanks" said Austin.

Austin helped Janice pick out a nice selection of poinsettias and carry them to the counter. Finally Janice broached the subject Austin had been afraid was coming. "So, did you do it? Did you call Mark?"

"I did, and he was great."

"I told you so. Are you going to keep seeing him?"

"I don't know. I– "

The back door flew open and Will burst in. "Austin. Oh Jesus. Oh God. Austin, you have to see!"

Will rubbed his hands across his face, pulling the skin

taut. His eyes were so wide, and his skin so pale he was almost comical, a parody of fear.

"Potting shed. Blood," he mumbled.

"Show me." Austin said.

Will turned and stumbled across the threshold. Both women followed him across the yard to the door of the potting shed. The same one that Austin had been locked in only three nights before.

The door was wide open. Will stood aside and the two women looked in.

Later, Austin would think how it had been like that painting in Mark's office. At first her mind just wouldn't let her see it, would not accept that the brown splotches and stains splattered across the bags of compost and fertilizer, puddled on the floor, and covering Bunny's blouse and hands, was dried blood. It took another moment for the fact to register that the wooden handle protruding from her throat was not attached to a knife, but to a simple everyday gardening implement, a trowel. It was the base of that trowel, painted white, slightly curved, that smiled at them from Bunny's throat. It was a thin-lipped smile, like the smile a child might draw, like the smile on one of those big yellow smiley face buttons.

Austin felt her mouth fill with saliva and knew she was going to be sick. She managed to take a few steps back before she had to bend over. Her stomach roiled and clenched. She swallowed hard and she could hear her ears ringing, but she did not get sick after all. After a few deep breaths she managed to stand upright. She turned to the others. Will was standing where he had stopped, far enough away so that he could not see inside the shed. His eyes were closed. Janice had backed up, as well. Her hands were clamped over her mouth and she was shaking her head back and forth.

"We need to call 911." Austin said. "We need to get the police."

Her words mobilized them.

"Should I shut the door?" Will asked.

"Was it open when you found it?"

"No. Closed and locked. I opened it." His expression clearly showed that he wished he hadn't.

"Leave it alone. Janice, come on. Let's get back inside the store."

Janice nodded and lowered her hands. Once inside, Austin dialed 911. The sound of a car pulling into the parking lot startled all of them.

"Put up the closed sign. Tell people we're. . .

Hello? This is Austin Ward, 2032 Spring Hill Road, Grace Gardens. I'm calling to report – to report a murder. Yes, that's right. Please send the police. No. I don't want to hang on. Just send the police." Austin hung up the phone. Her hands were trembling.

"The police are coming. I don't think we should do anything until they get here."

"I have to call my school, tell them I might not be back," said Janice.

Austin handed her the phone. Janice made her call and, as she was hanging up, they heard the sound of another car pulling into the parking lot.

Will went outside to tell them the nursery was closed.

Chapter 12

Sheriff's deputies were first to arrive on the scene. As one officer questioned them about what they had found, another began to string yellow tape around the potting shed. When Austin saw the tape, it made everything seem even less real. It was as if she had walked onto the set of some television crime drama.

She told the policeman who questioned her exactly what had happened but it felt as if she were somewhere outside herself, listening to the questions and answering in a wooden, emotionless voice. Why wasn't she crying? Shouldn't she be crying?

A pair of plainclothes detectives arrived, and Austin and Janice were taken to different areas of the nursery to be questioned again.

The one who led Austin to a corner of the store near the register was old enough to be her father, but her father had never been as grim and humorless. His faded blue eyes seemed to lock on hers, as if defying her to look away and signal her guilt. Without taking his eyes off her, he flipped open his notebook and took a pen from his shirt pocket.

"I'm Detective Clark with the Oregon State Police," he said, introducing himself. I want you to tell me everything that happened here today. I want you to take it slow, step by step, and as sequentially as you remember, OK?"

Somehow the firmness of his voice had a settling effect. Austin took a deep breath and began to recount the story, this time remembering to give Bunny's real name, Naomi. When the detective asked who owned the nursery and Austin said that she did, and that Bunny had worked for her, it felt a little like a confession. It was the situation, she decided. Being questioned, being so pointedly separated from the others, put her on the defensive.

He asked if all the employees had access to the shed.

Again, she felt guilty when she admitted that everyone did, and worse, that it was rarely locked anyway.

"Why is that?" he asked.

"We don't keep anything of value in it. Besides, I always lock the gate at the entrance when I leave."

"Do your employees have access to the gate?"

"Yes. They all have keys to the padlock."

"Is there any other way onto the property?"

"Well, it's not all fenced. The cyclone fence goes across the front of the parking area and along the sides and we lock the stock gate when we're closed, but the back is open. There's an irrigation ditch that runs along there and a row of brush and trees so you can't drive onto the property, but I suppose someone could walk in from there."

"What was Naomi's job?"

It took Austin a moment to remember who Naomi was, then she responded, "She was a clerk, mostly. Sometimes she helped with planting or feeding or watering, whatever needed to be done. We're too small to have any specialists."

"How did Naomi get along with the other employees? Did they like her?"

"Everyone liked Bunny," Austin said, truthfully.

"Was she married?"

"No."

"Involved with anyone?"

"She went out with different men."

"Do you know their names?"

"Some of them."

"And?"

"None of them killed her. They were all crazy about her."

"Then there's no harm in giving me their names."

"I didn't say I wouldn't." She was beginning to get annoyed. She thought a moment, then ran off the list of men that she knew Bunny had dated. "She was seeing Mike Bryant, He's a cook at the Blue Dolphin. Sometimes she went out with Lance Westerman, He works at the lumber mill, or at least he did. I think she dated a teacher at the high school, Paul something. Oh, and she was sort of dating one of her co-workers, Will Williams," she added reluctantly.

It wasn't until he asked where he could find Will that she realized he was gone. She was too confused to hide her surprise and when the detective saw it he stepped outside and got on his radio. It didn't take much reasoning for Austin to guess he was radioing a request for Will to be picked up. Will couldn't have done anything wrong, but the police wouldn't know that.

The detective returned and asked again if she had any

idea where Will could be found.

Austin repeated what she had said the first time. She had no idea where he was or why he had left. She had assumed he was out back speaking with one of the officers. He had gone outside to tell customers that they were closed. No, she couldn't remember seeing him after that.

She couldn't tell if the policemen believed her, but she realized she didn't really care all that much. At the moment all she wanted was for them to go away so she could be alone to think clearly. She was sure if she could just think for a moment she could puzzle out why Will would disappear like that.

An hour later, instead of leaving, the police allowed Austin and Janice to leave.

"I have your phone numbers, but please be sure to stay where I can reach you," the detective said to both of them, though it was Austin he was looking at when he said it. "I am sure I'll have more questions for both of you later. Also, would you mind telling me how you got that black eye?"

Austin raised her hand and touched the fading bruise around her eye. So much trouble, so many explanations.

They met at Austin's that night and filled her small living room with both their bodies and their anxiety. They sat on the couch in front of the fireplace or drew chairs up from the kitchen to huddle there, in front of that primitive source of warmth and comfort. Austin and Muncie, Janice, Paco and Josh, everyone but Will and, of course, Bunny.

"Who could have done it?" Janice was asking. "Someone who was going to rob the store? Was it a rapist? What did he want?"

"How many times do I have to tell you guys? It was

Will," demanded Muncie. "Otherwise, why would he have taken off like that?"

"It does look bad," agreed Austin. "But if you could have seen his face. He was as shocked as we were. Isn't that right, Janice?"

"Yes. He looked absolutely sick."

"Or he was doing a hell of a fine acting job," said Muncie. "I'll give him that. How much do we know about him? You ever meet his family? He have any friends?"

"I don't think his family lives around here. He's worked for me a little over two years and I've never met any of them or heard him talk about them, for that matter. He does have a couple friends. I've seen him with them in town, but he doesn't drag them to work with him. Why would he? He doesn't talk much anyway, so why would he tell me about his past if he doesn't even talk about the present? I just can't believe he's capable of something like this."

"Why?" asked Muncie. "Because he has a ponytail and wears round glasses and looks like a young John Lennon? Do you buy into that whole peace, love, hippie bullshit?"

"Of course not. I just think, well, he really loves plants. They respond to him and. . . "

"You know that's a really dumb argument," snapped Muncie, his voice shaking. Austin knew his anger masked concern. "You think, if someone likes plants that makes him a good person? How do you know Jack the Ripper wasn't a gardener? Couldn't someone who really likes plants hate people? I mean, maybe that's exactly why he liked working with plants in the first place. Think about it."

"Now you're starting to talk about him in the past tense, like he's gone forever or something," Austin said.

She slapped her hands on her knees and glared at him. "We don't know why he ran," she said, her voice rising to a shout. "He could have lots of reasons."

"Or just the one. Bunny."

They both fell silent.

Janice said, "This isn't a good time to let ourselves get upset."

Austin sighed, "She's right. The police said they thought they'd be through doing whatever they do in a few days. There's a medical examiner and a forensic unit coming in from Medford. What would you all say to closing up until after Christmas? There's only a few more yard cleanups scheduled. We can finish up this week and then take a break until mid-January. Paco, you and Josh can go ahead and file for unemployment."

"You could lose a lots of money," said Paco. "Christmas time we sell wreathes and Christmas flowers."

"I know but it just seems wrong. Celebrating Christmas. Making money. Shouldn't we be thinking about Bunny?"

"You can think about her, sure," said Muncie. "But you're a business person. You have people depending on you. You can't just close up because you feel like it."

"Don't be so mean," said Janice. "She's not saying she wants to quit. She's just upset that someone she knows just got killed and she, well, we three, saw her. You didn't see her. You don't know how horrible it was."

"I'm sorry. I don't mean to sound like such a hard ass. I just…well, I worry about her. She's my sister."

"I know." said Janice. She reached over and patted his arm. "I didn't mean to imply you didn't care."

"Hey, I'm still in the room, people." Austin reminded

them. "I know you're right, Muncie. I know I can't quit. I guess I just feel like I can't face going back there right now."

"You won't have to go back alone." said Janice. "Wait until someone can go with you."

"I'll go," said Josh. "Just give me a call."

"Yeah, your folks would love that," said Austin.

"I really have to move out of there," Josh said.

"Wouldn't make them worry less."

"I suppose," he acknowledged.

"It is more than money," said Paco, continuing where they had left it. "Remember, you told me last year if the customers learn you have the Christmas things they will return every year. If we are not there this year maybe they will not come again, yes?"

"Yes, I know you're probably right," Austin reluctantly agreed. "We are trying to build a customer base. Damn this mess! As soon as the police are done we'll open back up, though I doubt we'll have many customers once word of all this gets out."

"And you know it will," said Janice, reminding everyone how small a town Blue Spruce was, and how quickly and efficiently its grapevine worked. "I'm sure things will look better in the morning. We're all tired and upset and we all want things back the way they were. We don't want to believe some monster is out there killing people that we know and care about."

"But there is, and his name is Will," said Muncie.

"Muncie," said Austin sharply.

"Okay, okay, I won't say any more," Muncie said, holding his hands up in mock surrender. "It's late. I should be getting home anyway."

"It's too bad we don't have a butler," said Janice.

"What?" they all asked in unison.

"A butler. You know. They always find out the butler did it."

Muncie nodded. "A butler would be very handy right now."

"Well, we don't have one so we're going to just have to keep our minds open," Austin said, shooting a glance at Muncie, "and hope the police find out what happened. "I expect I'll be hearing from them in the morning. Maybe they'll have some answers by then. Anyway, I don't want to think about it anymore. I am exhausted. We all are. Get out of here and go home."

"Do you want a ride?" Paco asked Josh.

"Yes," Josh said. "Thanks."

After Paco and Josh drove away, Muncie and Janice each hugged Austin goodbye.

"You going to be okay?" Muncie asked.

"I'll be fine. I'm going straight to bed."

"Call if you can't sleep or anything," Janice said.

"I will," she promised.

She stepped out onto the porch to wave goodbye as they drove away. The wind was bitterly cold, and as soon as the last car's taillights disappeared she hurried back inside.

For all her brave words, the silence left by their departure felt overwhelming. Austin turned on the radio and, a few minutes later, the television as well. It was something she did when she felt particularly alone, as she did tonight.

She realized she was hungry and put together a peanut

butter and honey sandwich and poured a glass of milk.

After her simple dinner, she started a shower. As she stood under the hot spray she remembered another shower. Was it only a few nights ago? Four employees to worry about. That was what she had been thinking about then. And then there were three. And then there were three. The litany ran through her head, over and over.

All day she had held back, stayed in control. Now, from the pit of her stomach, a twisting, burning force gathered and broke in a deep sob. Tears spilled from her eyes. She stood under the shower, her face upraised, hot water and tears streaming, and let herself remember that Bunny, silly and vibrant and only twenty-one years old, was gone.

Chapter 13

On Wednesday morning a bar of golden sunlight fell in a warm rectangle across Austin's bed and her dozing form. She stretched and yawned, happy with the world, the blue sky framed by the window, the sound of a bird twittering outside. Then she remembered, and the memory of Bunny's death drove all the bright warmth away. She got up, moving slowly, as if her bones ached, and she was very tired. Her eyes were puffy and sore from crying.

There were so many things to take care of. She wanted to be sure the police had contacted Bunny's parents and she had to call, find out about the funeral, order flowers. She felt lost. She had no experience with this sort of thing. What was the proper etiquette when someone is murdered?

Of course she couldn't go to the nursery. The police hadn't said she could and besides, she didn't want to go there alone. It wasn't so much that she was afraid that some killer was hiding, watching. It was more that she was not ready to face the memory of finding Bunny, of seeing that smile slashed across her throat.

If Will hadn't disappeared, he would have gone with her. They would have been brave together. She was sure of Will, he had always been a gentle, quiet soul, someone she had worked alongside for over two years. Someone she could share comfortable silences with.

But what if Muncie was right? Could Will have killed Bunny? She didn't want to believe he was capable of murder, especially not in the horribly brutal way Bunny had been murdered.

Muncie would be working at his building site. Janice would be at work. Paco and Josh would be by to pick up the trailer soon. Maybe she should go out with them.

No, she decided, they didn't have a full day's work anyway and she was feeling tired and off-kilter, as if she'd like to cry or throw something. Better to spare them.

Maybe she needed some coffee. She headed into the kitchen to start a pot. The blinking red light on the answering machine caught her eye and she punched the button on her way by.

She heard her own voice saying, "Hello, you have reached Blue Spruce Landscaping. We are unavailable at the moment. Please leave your name and number and we will return your call as soon as possible."

"Hi, this is Blake. I just heard. I'm so sorry. Please call me."

She punched the button again, erasing the message, then jumped when the phone rang.

"Hello?" she said.

"Austin, it's Janice. How are you?"

"Fine, I guess."

"Busy today?"

"No. I have to make some calls. You know. Talk to Bunny's folks."

"How awful. Well, I made an appointment for you to see Mark today."

"What!"

"Now don't get all angry. You said yourself you hit it off fine with him and if ever you needed to talk with someone this would certainly be the time."

"But Janice, I don't want to deal with this right now."

"I don't think you have much choice in that, sweetheart. I'm so sorry, and the only way I can think to help is to get you to go see Mark again. Please. For me."

"You are such a pain."

"I know. Your appointment is at 1:30. Let me know how it goes."

"I will," Austin said, resignedly.

"Great. I love you."

"I love you too."

Austin hung up, less angry and more relieved than she'd expected. Maybe Mark could help. The sense of being mired in something beyond her ability to cope was awful. Maybe talking to him would help her put things in perspective. She decided not to call Blake. It was too early in their relationship to drag him into this kind of drama. She felt emotional and shaky. Not exactly the kind of image she wanted to project on a date.

After calling Bunny's parents and getting no answer Austin straightened the house, then showered and dressed for her appointment with Mark. She arrived just in time, and this time did not hesitate to open the door to 310 and step inside. In moments, Mark was ushering her into his office, and she sank into the brown recliner.

"You had a hell of a day yesterday," Mark said, not bothering with small talk.

"That's an understatement," Austin said.

Mark swiveled his chair so it was facing hers and sat down. They were only inches apart. She looked up into dark brown eyes, noted his furrowed brow and, for no reason she could name, began to cry. Wordlessly, he handed her the box of Kleenex he kept nearby. She smiled, a nervous twitch of her lips that held more pain than mirth, and wiped her eyes.

She told him about finding Bunny. About the tragedy of losing someone who was so young. She talked about her anger at death and how unjust it all seemed. She even told him about her father's death. How he had flown his Piper Cub into the side of a mountain.

"Everyone said it was an accident. That Dad was getting old and maybe he wasn't as sharp as he should have been. That was bullshit. The only thing wrong with Dad was missing Mom. After she died he just started to fade away. We always thought, me and my brother I mean, we always wondered if it was an accident or whether he was he just tired of being alone."

"He had you and your brother."

"Not the same. Him and Mom had something special, a connection. Maybe it was all that traveling together. New places, new people, they sort of anchored each other, you know? When Dad died he left me some money. I used it to buy the nursery and I named it after her, Grace Gardens. I think he would have liked that."

"I'm sure he would."

Later, the sound of the front office buzzer startled

Austin, and when she looked at her watch she saw that nearly two hours had gone by. It was remarkable to her that she could spend so much time talking about herself.

She stood, and Mark took her jacket from the couch, where she'd tossed it, and held it for her. As she pulled it on she fought the urge to turn and press herself into his arms. She had seen therapists before and knew that the closeness was artificial, a mock intimacy, one that helped break through a client's reserve but would not, and probably should not, survive outside of their sessions. She buttoned her coat, turned and said goodbye and thank you instead.

When she got home she would call Blake. Obviously she needed someone. She might as well try and find out if he was that someone.

Chapter 14

Late Friday morning the police told Austin she could reopen the nursery. The investigation was continuing, but if she kept clear of the cordoned-off potting shed, she and her employees could return to work.

She called both Paco and Josh and told them she planned to reopen on Tuesday and might need their help, but she didn't want to cause them problems with their unemployment claims.

"You signed on to do lawn maintenance, not work the nursery," she told them. "But if you are willing to, and if I could promise you full-time work, I'd keep you on. The problem is I was about to cut Bunny's hours, and I can only promise a few hours here and there. I think you'd be better off drawing unemployment or looking for something else to get you through the winter."

"I'll hold off filing for unemployment until after you tell me you don't need anyone," offered Josh. "Let Paco go ahead. He's got a family."

"That's thoughtful of you," Austin said, grateful for Josh's attitude. She had never paid "under the table" the way many of the small local businesses were forced to. Partly because she was intimidated by the idea of getting in trouble with the state or the IRS, and partly because she wanted to prove to herself that she could make it without having to submit to those kinds of practices.

After she hung up she decided she had to face it. She had to go to the nursery. She knew Muncie would be angry that she hadn't waited and asked him to go with her, but she knew she felt stronger since her session with Mark. Besides, she would rather be alone to deal with whatever emotions being there might stir up.

As she drove she thought about Josh. He lived with his parents on a sheep ranch just over the hill behind Austin's house. She'd met his parents several times. They were in their late sixties. Josh had been a late-in-life baby. A complete surprise to the Mikkelsons, who had decided it was God's desire that they remain childless. This did not stop them from fostering one after another of their nephews and nieces.

Because the Mikkelson clan was, aside from Josh's parents, extremely fertile, there were many, many cousins for Josh to grow up with. Usually, they were troubled kids, sent to the sheep ranch as a last attempt to get them to straighten out. From what Josh said, the arrangement had worked out well.

Josh made no secret of his belief that his parents were old-fashioned and hopelessly rule-bound, but he also liked to brag that they were the most successful foster parents in the state.

"You know," he had told Austin once, "If they paid my folks the money the state saves on jail time for some of those dumb-ass cousins of mine, they'd be rich."

Austin thought it was this somewhat unusual

upbringing that gave Josh the opposing sides of his nature. He had his rebellious side, the side that had him smoking cigarettes (when he knew it drove his parents crazy), and his responsible side, which made sure he was never late for work. She thought it would be interesting to see which side ended up winning; probably neither. No one is all one thing, she decided, as she cautiously pulled around and passed a truck hauling a load of logs.

The sky was overcast, with thick gray clouds slashed and tattered by the wind. The air smelled like snow. It would be strange to return to the nursery. She wondered if the image of Bunny would always be waiting there.

She had to unlock the front gate, swing it open, drive through and then close and lock it behind her. She parked in front of the store, climbed out, and as her gloved fingers fumbled with the key, she began to reconsider whether she should call Muncie.

She had sort of half-promised to take him with her. He was going to be ticked off. Besides, she had to admit she felt a little nervous. Company would make her feel safer. Then she firmly dismissed the idea. If she kept calling Muncie every time she felt uncomfortable or had a bad moment, he would never leave. He belonged in Portland, working on a degree in architecture. He shouldn't be living in a small town, barely getting by, wasting his life taking care of his little sister.

Ever since Muncie's break up with Debbie, Austin had worried that it was her leaving Denver that had been the cause. Sure, she had never liked Debbie but still it bothered her that Muncie and Debbie's relationship seemed to unravel so quickly right after Austin announced her decision to move to Oregon. It had been a simple decision. She'd been accepted by the college she wanted to attend, she'd never seen Oregon, and that was that.

She hadn't really thought about the fact that Muncie had worried about her, lived near her, and always tried to care for her ever since the night he and his friend had accidentally locked her in a bomb shelter.

Austin was only seven then, yet she still remembered it. Or maybe she had played that memory over so many times that what she believed and reality had nothing to do with each other. How could she be sure? Memory was a funny thing. Sometimes the sound of a shoe squeaking against a hardwood or linoleum floor would be enough to trigger it. She remembered that, the slap and squeal of sneakers and the high-pitched shouts of their young voices echoing from the basement hallway's brick walls. In the ceiling, the long panel of fluorescent lights flickering furiously, as if in protest against the noise.

They raced down the hall, pounding toward the finish line. Her brother and his friend, Brian in front, side by side, when suddenly Muncie tripped. Running close behind, she had fallen across her brother's prone body in a sprawling heap.

Without hesitation Brian leapt aside, kept running, and seconds later slapped his hands triumphantly on the steel door at the end of the hall.

"Not fair. I stepped on my shoelace," declared Muncie, pushing Austin away impatiently and climbing to his feet.

"Your problem," said Brian. He turned from the door, an elfish grin on his face. He was tall for his age and bone-thin, with blond, almost white hair, light green eyes, and a pointed chin.

She pushed herself away from her brother, sliding backward on her rear until she came up against the wall, where she sat, glaring at the boys, an expression of pure contempt in her dark brown eyes. Her dress was rumpled, and one of her socks had slid down her leg to bunch around a pale ankle.

"Yeah, well, let's do something else," suggested her brother. "I'm bored."

Austin had pushed sweat-dampened bangs off her forehead. "We could play hopscotch," she suggested.

"Right, Austin." Her brother rolled his eyes. "That sounds sooo exciting."

"So what do you want to do, if you're so smart?"

"I don't know," he admitted.

"Hey, I know," suggested Brian. "Let's explore the shelter."

"We're not supposed to," she'd said, still hoping they might change their minds and play hopscotch. She had just learned how, and wanted to play every waking moment. Only there weren't any girls her age in the building, and since the bad weather started, she hadn't been allowed outside. Her warning had exactly the opposite effect she was hoping for. The boys had become even more enthusiastic about their plan.

The place they wanted to explore was a bomb shelter, a cold war relic. The entrance to it was at the end of the hall. Cut into the brick wall was an opening four feet wide and six feet tall. Its threshold two feet above the floor was a perfect perch for kids.

The thick metal door to the shelter had been tied open, ensuring that no one could get inside, close the door, and become trapped.

Standing just outside the entrance, they could see only a few feet into the hole, just as far as the hallway's fluorescent lights could reach. That light revealed a dirt floor strewn with empty chocolate milk cartons, candy bar wrappers, and other bits of garbage. Beyond that, nothing, only utter darkness, and whatever your imagination could create. That was what made the shelter, the big hole-in-the-wall, both scary and intriguing.

They gathered near the shelter. Austin reached inside and smoothed a small section of the cool dirt floor, careful to avoid a cheeseburger wrapper, and absently began to sketch a tic-tac-toe grid with her finger.

"My dad told me this is where we would go if there's a war and they send bombs at us," Muncie had said.

"I know," Brian had agreed. "My dad said when you shut the door, lights come on, and big secret panels in the walls open up, and there's all kinds of stuff."

"Like what?" Muncie had asked.

"Like beds and food rations and water. Stuff like that."

"That would be cool." Muncie said.

"The children looked longingly into the mysterious black hole.

"You know," said Brian, "I bet we could shut it."

They moved back to examine the door. A wire, about the thickness of a coat hanger, had been looped around the door handle, passed through the eye of a large bolt in the wall a few times, and then twisted together. The door was thick—a good eight inches of heavy steel, with strong, spring-loaded hinges meant to assist in its closing. Only three slightly rusty twists of wire were keeping it open. If they could untwist those strands, the door would close.

They couldn't reach it. They weren't tall enough. They tried jumping for it but it was too high, even for Brian, the tallest of them, to reach. Austin and her brother knelt on the floor and let Brian stand on their backs, but still he could only barely touch the wire with his fingertips.

If there had been anything else to do, they might have given up. But with the snow, and the cold, and no school because it was Christmas break, they had little to distract them.

"We need a ladder," Brian said. "Let's see if we can find one."

The boys galloped down the hall toward the laundry room, while Austin took her hopscotch necklace out of her pocket and tossed it half-heartedly onto the linoleum. The pattern of alternating dark and light colored squares made it the perfect floor for hopscotch. She sighed heavily, scooped up her necklace, and hurried to catch up with the boys.

The laundry room was steamy and warm from the long banks of chugging, swishing washing machines and dryers. At one of the narrow folding tables in the center aisle, two women—the children's mothers—chatted and played gin rummy. Every so often one of them would get up and move a load of laundry from washer to dryer, or fold a few pieces of clothing and place them in a basket to be hauled upstairs later.

"Hey mom," Brian said, tugging on his mother's sleeve. "Can we use that chair?"

He pointed to one of several chairs placed randomly around the tables.

"What do you want it for?" she asked.

"We need it for a game."

"I don't think so. What if you fell off and got hurt? Your father would be upset."

"Fine," Brian said, in a voice that said nothing was fine. He stomped away and began to kick morosely at the cement-lined trough that held the washers.

Austin asked her mom for a drink. She took a sip of her mother's soda and placed the bottle carefully back on the table. She did not spill or drop things hardly ever anymore. She was a big girl, just turned seven.

Muncie, who was two years older and somewhat wiser in the ways of getting around parental restrictions, didn't ask for permission. He simply began to scoot a small table he'd spotted just inside the laundry room, a table no one used because it was missing one of its legs, out into the hallway. No one noticed.

Once in the hallway, the table slid easily along the waxed floor. Before Muncie had pushed it halfway to its destination, Austin and Brian had seen what he was doing and bolted down the hall to help. The table slid even faster when they all pushed.

Once the table was in place below the shelter's door, Brian tried to climb on top of it but it immediately tipped.

"Whoa," he said, grabbing the wire to steady himself.

Austin and Muncie moved forward, pushed the table firmly against the wall and held it there.

Brian held on to the wire with his left hand and carefully reached up with his right to try and untwist the ends. The wire was much stronger, and more tightly wound, than he had expected. It barely moved.

"We need a knife or something flat we can stick in here," he'd told them.

Austin let go of the table and reached into her pocket. The hopscotch chain was there, and attached to it was a set of dog tags. Her dad had them made up for her at the Post Exchange. The dog tags were thin rectangles of tin, similar to her father's real tags, but with her name and birth date printed on them.

"Here," she said.

Brian leaned down and took them from her. He used the corner of one of the metal tags to chip away some of the rust and then forced the thin plate between the wires. The tag bent with the strain but he kept pushing and twisting and finally, with a thin creaking sound, the strands of wire began to part.

"Hey, if the door closes we won't be able to see what happens inside," observed Muncie.

"You're right," said Brian. "One of us has to go inside."

"Well I can't, I'm holding the table," said Muncie.

They both looked at Austin. "But I don't want to," she said.

"Why not?" asked her brother. "Don't you want to see the room with all the stuff inside? Come on. It'll be fun."

"You do it," she said.

"I can't. I have to hold the table or it'll fall over."

Brian leapt down from the table. "Come on," he said. Then taunting; "What are you, a scaredy cat?"

"No."

"Are too."

"I am not."

"Are too. All girls are stupid chicken scaredy cats."

"They are not."

"And billy ittle sitches, too."

They were suddenly silent. Billy ittle sitches. Silly little bitches, it was an expression Brian had taught Muncie. Austin knew it was a bad thing to say, every bit as bad as the "F" word. It was the kind of thing you only said to your worst enemy or when you hit your head really hard and, even then, only when there were no adults around.

Austin wrinkled her nose and wailed. "I'm going to tell. You called me a bad word and I'm going to tell my m-mother." She turned and began to stomp away.

"Wait," Brian called. "Don't you go telling your mom. Come on, you don't want to be a tattletale."

"Yeah," said her brother. "Tattletale."

"I'll play hopscotch with you," Brian shouted.

Austin stopped and turned around.

"I mean it," he promised. "I'll play hopscotch with you. You just go in and see what's in there and then we'll play hopscotch. We both will, won't we?" he asked Muncie.

"Sure," her brother promised, unconvincingly.

Shaking herself free of the memory, Austin thought that it was his failed promise to open the door that kept Muncie worried about her and made him feel like he had to take care of her. Soon after his breakup with Debbie, he had shown up on her doorstep in Portland with luggage and a bag of carpenter's tools. He said he had left his wife and didn't want to talk about it.

Within a week he had a job. A month later they were sharing a much nicer apartment than the one she'd been able to afford as a student. She never asked if part of his decision to leave Debbie was so that he could follow her to Oregon and keep an eye on her, his slightly damaged sister. She didn't really want to know.

After graduation, Muncie had helped her move to Blue Spruce, the town that her best friend from college called home. Since one town was as good as another to Austin, it hadn't taken much for Janice to talk her into moving there. The plan had been that she and Janice would find teaching jobs, maybe even at the same school.

Once she was hired as a substitute, however, it quickly became apparent to Austin that she hated working inside all day. The rooms seemed stifling, and though she liked children in ones and twos, she didn't really enjoy them in large groups.

She found a part-time job, helping out at a plant nursery and then quit substituting altogether and took a job working for a landscaper she met at the nursery. After deciding she could do a better job, and sick of the married owner hitting on her, she decided to start a lawn care company of her own.

By the end of her second summer she knew she was going to do all right. She had more customers than she could handle, and had found work she really enjoyed. Then Muncie appeared, again with a couple duffel bags and his tools. This time he got his own apartment and she eventually rented a house. She didn't want to live with her brother anymore. She wanted to feel like an adult.

However, when their parents died within months of each other, she had been grateful that he was so close. She didn't know how she could have managed dealing with everything without him. She hated to lean on him, didn't expect his help with the myriad problems the nursery, the landscaping business, and her own fixer upper home entailed. Still, she knew that she had needed him, at least in the beginning, but that was over now. She'd taken all the help she'd cared to. It was time to let Muncie get on with his own life.

Austin finally got the key into the lock and slid the door open. The scent of pine, cedar, soil and herbicide met her like old friends. She inhaled deeply and sighed, reaching for the light switch. The double bank of fluorescent lights drove away the shadows. It was all so mundane, so anticlimactically quiet.

She spent the rest of the morning going through a stack of invoices. At lunchtime she closed up and drove to town for a sandwich and a soda. She knew it was an expensive habit, not fixing her own lunch, but thought she'd earned a reward for dealing with the paperwork.

When she got back she decided to check the greenhouses. The trees, bulbs and tubers that were being stored there had to be kept at the right humidity and temperature levels. With a glance at the dismal sky, she opened the back door of the store.

Yellow tape still dangled from one corner of the potting shed. The wind picked it up and wound it, like a thin scarf, around a stack of ceramic pots. Austin, hunched inside her coat, hurried past.

She found the humidity and temperature of the greenhouses within tolerable levels, so she continued past them to the rows of trees and shrubs.

The past owners had put in forsythia, lilac, flowering crab apples, and other ornamentals. There were also several rows of arborvitae, dwarf junipers, and badly shaped three-year-old pines and firs.

Austin planned to expand the ornamentals, wait and see what the demand was for the rest. She'd also been considering another greenhouse she could devote to growing houseplants. The jade she supplied to local stores was selling pretty well.

The first big flakes began to fall while she was at the northeast edge of the property. She'd been staring down at the muddy trickle of water at the bottom of the irrigation canal that bordered it. She was thinking about whether she should buy a new pump now or wait for the old wheezing one to die completely.

When she felt the first flake fall on her eyelash, she blinked and looked up. The sky was filled with pivoting flakes of snow. Delighted, Austin threw back her head and watched it come down. So what if the roads got slippery and they couldn't work. So what if three months from now she was cursing this stuff. Right here and right now she was as thrilled and as filled with wonder as a child.

Unobserved, she felt free to hold her arms away from her sides and spin slowly, the motion making the flakes look even more frenzied as they danced in answer to the wind.

Soon her hair and face were damp and dotted with melting snowflakes. Finally, she lowered her arms and, with a wide smile on her face, turned her back to the rising wind and walked back to the store.

As she caught sight of the edge of the potting shed she thought of Bunny and felt a rush of guilt at the joy she had been feeling. Poor Bunny would never feel snow on her face again.

The heat shimmering in the air in front of the wall heater was welcome. Austin hung up her parka and held her hands out to warm them. The snow quickly melted and her face soon felt too hot and tight. She moved away from the heater and resumed the tedious chore of paperwork.

She put together a pile of receipts to copy and filled out her quarterly tax statement. She was pleased with how much easier it seemed than last time. Maybe she could learn not to totally hate the accounting stuff. She was just finishing up when a noise outside startled her.

She jerked upright, and swiveled around on the stool

she'd been using. What was that? This time she recognized the sound. Footsteps. Someone was walking across the parking lot, footsteps crunching through the gravel. She'd closed the stock gate behind her when she drove in. She knew the big "Closed" sign they'd hung on the gate was still there, so who would be walking up to the store and how did they get in?

A sharp memory of Bunny flashed through Austin's mind: Bunny arched across sacks of peat moss, her eyes sunken holes in her pale face, the disturbing line of the trowel buried in her throat.

Austin swallowed hard and looked around for a weapon. Lying on the counter near the register was one of the utility knives they used to open boxes. Her fingers trembled as she fumbled to pick it up. It was small, with a slim plastic handle and a narrow, razor-sharp blade that retracted into the handle. It didn't look like much of a weapon, but she knew from experience it could cut deeply and painfully. Of course, cutting herself by mistake was one thing; cutting another human being was something entirely different.

A dark, wide-shouldered form loomed into sight just outside the sliding glass doors. Abruptly, the door slid aside.

"Austin."

"Will?" Austin recognized the voice but not the body. Then he stepped into the light and she realized he was wearing a heavy parka, his thin frame disguised by its bulk.

"I saw the lights. I was hoping it was you."

Her heart beating wildly, Austin swallowed and tightened her grip on the knife she was holding just below the level of the counter. Slowly, soundlessly she slid the blade out.

"What's wrong?"

"Where have you been?" she managed to croak.

"Hiding."

"Why? Do you know what everyone thinks?"

"That I killed Bunny, I suppose. But you know I didn't."

"I want to believe you didn't. But why did you run?"

"The police. Look, there's a warrant out for my arrest. I couldn't let the police ID me. The warrant would pop up and that would be it. I'd go to jail."

"A warrant? For what?"

"It wasn't any big deal. I didn't rob a bank or anything. It's just– sort of complicated – hard to explain."

"Try," Austin insisted, her palm sweating where it gripped the knife.

"I stole a car. This was in California about two years ago. I figured Oregon wouldn't go to the expense of tracking down someone with a California warrant for something as lame as that, so I hitched up here, you were hiring, and that was it. See? No big deal. I've been careful not to get busted for anything else, but I knew if the cops ran my name through their database that warrant would pop up, and they'd have me."

"Wouldn't that be better than having them think you're a killer?"

"I guess I thought they'd find the killer right away and after a while I could show back up and everything would be fine."

"That was smart," she said sarcastically.

"I know. I know." Will agreed. "I've decided to turn myself in. I just – I'm sort of freaked out about it. I guess I should call a lawyer or something."

"Well at least you are starting to think. I have a customer who's become a friend. Her son is a criminal lawyer. I suppose I could try to contact him," offered Austin.

"Really? That would be great. It would be a lot easier than just walking into the police station."

"We'll go to my house and I'll look her number. You can call her from there."

"That would be great.

"Where have you been hiding?"

"Around."

He had moved across the room to a table covered with plants. His fingers moved across the rows of poinsettias, deftly removing dead leaves, probing the soil for moisture. She remembered the day the clippings had arrived from Los Angeles, the care with which he had planted each one.

"Will."

"Don't tell anyone, okay? I have a friend who works at the U-Haul place. He left the back of one of the trucks open and I've been sleeping in there."

"You must have been freezing."

"No, it's an old broke down truck where they store the blankets they rent for padding furniture. I just sort of made a nest in there and it was fine. I just made sure I woke up early enough to be gone before people started showing up."

"Well, that explains where you slept, but how did you stay out of sight during the day?"

"Well I still have keys to everything. The greenhouses are nice and warm"

"You were here?" Austin shook her head in disbelief.

"Well, I suppose if you were going to kill me you could have done it by now."

"Yeah, 'specially when you were spinning around like a top with your tongue stuck out catching snow flakes."

"Yeah, well maybe I shouldn't call my friend after all. Maybe you should just march your butt down to the police station."

"Ah, Austin, come on. You shouldn't be like that."

Austin laughed. Suddenly she knew that Will was innocent. She was convinced that his story, despite how dumb it sounded, no, because of how dumb it sounded, was true. Under cover of the counter, she slid the blade back into the box knife's handle and slipped it into the back pocket of her jeans.

With an overwhelming sense of relief she said, "Let's lock up and go get you some dinner. I know you're probably scared but I don't think it'll be as bad as you think. At least you'll be turning yourself in. That has to count for something."

"It does in the movies. Only, this ain't no movie."

"No, it sure isn't. We'll just have to hope for the best."

Chapter 15

As soon as they were safely inside Austin's house, Will hurried to shut the living room drapes, while Austin went around the room turning on lights.

Will was nervous, pacing from window to window, peering out at the street. Austin turned on the oven to preheat it and pulled a pizza out of the freezer. She also took a couple of beers out of the fridge and handed him one, hoping it might help calm him.

"You need to settle down." she said. "You haven't changed your mind have you? You still want me to call my friend, right?"

"Yes. I'm just messed up about all this. People thinking I killed Bunny. My dad will. . . well he won't be surprised. He was probably expecting something like this."

"Your dad?"

Will took a deep breath. "Nine years ago, when I was seventeen, I lived with my father. The Honorable William Williams."

"Williams? Senator William Williams?" Austin asked

"You know three people named William Williams?"

"Don't be a smart ass."

"Admit it. It's a pretty unusual name. I always thought you'd put two and two together."

"And get five. Which must be what happened here, because I certainly never put Will Williams and Senator William Williams together," Austin admitted.

"Yeah, I can see that. Why would you. I don't much take after the old man." He paused to take a long drink. Wiping his mouth with the back of his hand, he said, "When I was seventeen I borrowed my father's Mercedes and had an accident. It wasn't a big deal. I misjudged the distance and smacked into a lamp pole in a parking lot. I wasn't traveling fast, so it didn't do a hell of a lot of damage. I bumped my head on this thing clipped to the visor, an insurance cardholder or whatever. It had a sharp corner and I bled like crazy. The police put me in an ambulance and made me go to the hospital, although I knew I was fine.

"I was sitting there, blood still all over me, holding a big gauze thing on my head when my father walks in. He sees me and guess what he says?"

"Are you all right?" Austin guessed.

"Hell no. He said, 'Do you know how much that car cost?' Will took another drink and then, with a thin smile pulling at his lips he said, "That's right. No, 'How you doing?' No, 'You gonna live?' Nope. Just, 'Do you know how much that car cost?' And then some crap about insurance rates and what will the newspapers make of it. I was already shutting him out by then."

"Maybe you misunderstood. People handle things different ways. I mean, maybe they had already told him

111

you were okay."

Will shrugged. "Maybe, and maybe I would have let it go, but he made such a big thing out of me messing up his car. He wouldn't let it drop. He made me get drug tested. He made them screen for alcohol, marijuana, cocaine, speed, and heroine. I remember because the screening place would only do three substances for some base rate, so he had to pay extra. He was pissed off about that too. Like it was my idea."

"Maybe he was just worried about you."

"He was worried I'd screw up his political career. You should have seen what it was like to live with him. You couldn't fart in your own house. He didn't give a damn about anything but how things looked. It was all about image. You've read about how shallow actors and politicians are. Do you think that's all some kind of urban myth? It's not." He took another sip of beer before continuing.

"My mom died when I was thirteen," he said, "I hardly remember her. Sometimes I don't think she died so much as just faded out of sight. I think maybe he just ignored her to death."

"That is such a sad, kind of creepy, thing to say," said Austin.

"I guess. But that's how it seemed. We never talked about her. It was like she never existed at all. We got along fine until the school thing. I wanted to major in botany and he wanted me to go to law school. Law school! How the hell was I supposed to do that? But I said I would. He made me promise I would. I tore up the catalogs from the school I was planning to apply to. I applied to that hell-hole he wanted me to go to. I mean, couldn't he see I was just handing him my whole future? That was like a week before the accident so it wasn't like I was being a hard-ass or anything. I was giving him just what he wanted. So did I deserve the drug tests? It was awful. I had to stand there and pee while some perverted bastard stared at my. . .well, you know." He finished off his beer and set it on the coffee table.

Austin couldn't think of what to say.

"I was mad," Will continued. "First chance I got I stole his keys, took the Mercedes to the top of this road up in the hills, started it up, put it in gear, jumped out and let it roll right over the side of a cliff. I figured it would blow up like on TV. Only it didn't happen like that. It just rolled down the hill, sort of slow, got hung up on a bush and almost stopped. Then it got going a little, hit a tree and turned over on its roof and then it slid sort of slowly the rest of the way. It just laid there at the bottom, wheels still turning, engine still going for a while. It was pretty much a let-down. I mean, I was expecting fireworks and the thing was like a big, fat turtle stuck on its back." Will smiled but there was no humor in it.

After a while I climbed down the hill and shut it off. I took the keys and kept them. I'm not really sure why." He reached into the neck of his T-shirt and pulled out a key suspended from a leather cord.

"I went back home but the head housekeeper, she and I were friends, we'd sneak in the garage with the gardener and smoke a little weed now and then. Anyway, she warned me Dad had called the police and that they'd issued a warrant for my arrest for grand theft auto. I guess it's a felony if the car is worth over a certain amount. Doesn't pay to have good taste. I borrowed some money and took off. I hitchhiked north and wound up here and I've been here ever since. I didn't think California would waste money trying to get me to come back for such a minor charge, and I knew Oregon wouldn't do California any favors, so I decided I was pretty safe."

"Well, that's an interesting way to look at it. But you're probably right. Plus, your father probably wouldn't have followed through with it. You said he didn't want to mess up his career. How would having your son be a convicted felon look?"

"I know. I realized that later, but so what. I don't want or need the old man's money. I don't need his lifestyle or the crap that comes with it. I just want to be left alone."

"I can see that, but with Bunny's murder and . . . what is it?"

Will had come to his feet in one fluid motion and slipped across the room until he was poised near the kitchen door, as if ready to bolt out the back.

Then Austin heard it too. "It's just a car pulling in," she said. "Let me see who it is."

"You called the police."

"That's right. All the time I was talking to you I was secretly dialing the police with my toes, or maybe sending Morse code telepathically."

"Yeah, well, okay. But who could it be?"

"Gee, let me think; a friend, a neighbor, one of the crew? How should I know? You stay there while I find out."

Austin moved to the living room's picture window, pulled aside the edge of one of the drapes and peeked out.

"It's Muncie," she declared.

"Should I hide?" asked Will

"I don't know. I suppose so. You're not his favorite

person right this minute. You can hide in the guestroom. It's down the hall, first door on the right. Stay there until he leaves. And be quiet."

Will slipped into the guestroom and pulled the door closed behind him, just before Austin heard the familiar knock on her front door. She opened it and stood aside as her brother strode in, pulling off his gloves.

"Hey, where you been? I called earlier," he said, moving past her into the living room.

"Went to the nursery to do some work." Austin turned and noticed that her and Will's beer bottles were sitting on the coffee table. She picked them both up and carried them to the kitchen. "I'm turning into the world's biggest slob these days," she said apologetically.

"Or a raging alcoholic."

"That too."

"I'm surprised you went back to the nursery all by yourself," said Muncie.

"I'm a big girl, you know."

"Yeah, but it must have been pretty scary."

"It was, sort of. At first I kept hearing noises but it was just my imagination. So, why were you trying to reach me?"

"Oh, this house I'm working on, the one by the lake. I'm going to be out there tomorrow. I know it's Saturday, but I thought maybe you could drop by. The owner would like an opinion on the landscaping. Maybe he'll even hire you to design the whole thing. He's got the money."

"Well, as you know, my social calendar is pretty full on Saturdays, but I suppose I could squeeze it in. What time?"

"How about eleven? Then we could go to lunch afterwards?"

"Sounds good to me. Well, I hate to kick you out, but I'm really tired."

"Me too. So, I'll see you tomorrow?" Muncie asked.

Putting her hand over her mouth to stifle a yawn, she said, "Sure. Tomorrow."

Austin waited until she heard Muncie's car pull out of the driveway, than opened the door to the guest room, a misnomer for a room that contained nothing but some empty packing boxes and an ironing board.

The room was empty. Will was gone. One corner of the curtain was stuck under the window. Austin freed it. He must have opened the window, climbed out, then closed the window behind him before running away. Austin stared up at the sky. The wind had swept the clouds away, which meant the night would be bitterly cold. Why had he run this time, she wondered. Had he told her the truth?

No, she wasn't going to ride that seesaw. The story he'd told her sounded weird enough to be true. He really was trying to avoid going to jail for stealing and wrecking his father's car. It was too stupid and too sad. He had sounded so ready to give himself up to the police, to clear himself of the murder of Bunny.

Had talking about his father reminded Will too much of the past? Did his running have less to do with facing the police than with facing his father? Austin was sure her guess was right. Until Will was ready to do that, he would just keep running.

She poured the remains of their beers down the kitchen drain. The smell made her queasy. She remembered she hadn't eaten all day.

Unwrapping the partly thawed pizza she began to think about Blake's invitation to dinner. She had promised to call him. What was she so worried about, she wondered: that this relationship would never make it, or that it would? Was she too independent? Too happy doing things her own way? She slid the pizza into the oven. The prospect of another night spent eating an unappetizing dinner alone then going to bed with some late night TV show for company was getting old. She decided she would call Blake, soon.

Chapter 16

Austin spent a few moments considering the amount of housework she had to do and decided that meeting Muncie at the Lake House early was a valid excuse for not doing it.

They had named the house Muncie was building at the lake "The Lake House," then laughed at their lack of creativity. It was as close to her ideal house as Austin could imagine. She wouldn't mind wandering through it again, pretending it was being built for her. She knew she shouldn't let herself fall in love with it. After all, she had her own house and, for all its chipped paint and scratched floors, it had its good points: hardwood floors, a view of the valley. But she had to admit, The Lake House could easily seduce her into being unfaithful.

The house sat perched all by itself on a mini-peninsula that jutted into the lake. Austin drove up the narrow road, that wound through a forest of pine, juniper, and low growing bitterbrush, and on around the curving driveway, edged with blocks of natural stone, to the front of the house.

As she pulled up, she noticed that the windows were installed and the cedar siding was up. From the outside the house appeared nearly complete, and even the dock was in place. A private dock, now *that* would be nice to own, she decided.

She parked behind Muncie's battered red and white Ford pickup, with its distinctive oversized contractor's tool box, and the ladder racks he'd proudly welded together by himself. She switched off the ignition and gave herself a moment to take in the sweeping vista of the lake and the mist-shrouded hills on the far side.

Beyond the hills, as if it were floating in the sky, was the snow-capped top of Mt. McLaughlin. She could only imagine what effect waking up to that view every morning would have on a person. It would be a little like waking up inside a really good dream. Of course you'd eventually realize it wasn't a dream, so maybe not so great after all. She smiled at her ability to find sour grapes and let go of envy.

Sighing, she climbed out of her truck, taking her clipboard with her. She planned to sketch the general layout of the grounds, then take the drawing home and do them on her computer. She had a great new software program that promised to turn her ideas into a professional-looking presentation, and she was dying to try it out on a real job.

The cold, moist wind coming off the lake tore through her coat and Austin was glad to find the front door of the house unlocked. She ducked inside, out of the wind, and was immediately assailed by the smells of sawdust, sheetrock dust and propane fumes. In the center of the living room, in front of the massive stone fireplace, her brother's propane heater was roaring, a sheet of controlled but still fearsome flame jetting loudly from one end of it.

"Hey, anyone here?" she called.

There was no answer, but she wasn't surprised. The place was huge, the heater loud enough to drown out her voice. She looked up at the 24-foot high ceiling, admiring the open beams and imagining how things would look, once stain, and paint, and carpet were in place. The walls were up and taped but not yet textured and the floor was nothing but wide stretches of plywood.

She wandered into the kitchen, calling Muncie's name as she went. She spotted the door to the basement standing ajar and opened it wider. "Hey, you down there?" she called.

Getting no answer, and realizing how dark it was below, she began to close the door. She never finished the movement. A hard shove between her shoulder blades sent her forward. She rammed, shoulder first, into the edge of the door jamb, then stumbled toward the steep stairs.

Austin threw her hands up reflexively and her right hand caught the stair rail. She twisted, momentum half turning her, and slammed shoulder first into the wall. Her left hand joined her right in grasping the rail, and as soon as she felt stable she looked up to see who had pushed her. He was no more than a shadow, a distorted shape, surrounded by a corona of light.

She watched in horror as the light that had framed him abruptly shrank to a narrow vertical band and then was gone. The sound of the slamming door echoed through the basementr and seemed to reverberate inside her head. She closed her eyes. A bright yellow rectangle filled the space behind her eyelids. Maybe she could convince herself it was light and not just an afterimage. Maybe she could pretend this was just a game. Muncie must be playing a joke. That was all. He'd open the door any minute and say something sarcastic and funny. Only she knew that Muncie would never do such a thing. He knew her. He knew her fears. So where was he, and who was that, up there?

She made her way to the landing and realized she'd only stumbled down two steps before catching herself. She reached through the darkness for the door. When she let go of the railing, the room seemed to spin around her, the landing to shift beneath her feet. Her hands found the door and slid across its smooth surface until she found the doorknob. She wrapped her hands around it, tried to turn it. She wasn't surprised to find the door was locked. She tugged on it. The door was new and her brother, damn his competence, had hung it. It barely moved.

The room grew hot. Not warm. Hot. She tried to take a deep breath but there wasn't enough air and the room was spinning faster now. It was as if her hands on the doorknob were her only point of connection in the center of a whirling vortex, a vortex that was trying to pull her into the darkness, to throw her down the stairs, where it waited to swallow her whole. She could hear it down there, waiting, breathing, a hungry darkness whose power grew while hers waned. She couldn't fight, couldn't breathe. The doorknob was slick with sweat. Her hands were slipping. The room was turning, twisting. She fell into darkness.

Chapter 17

Austin's next conscious thought was to note how bright the sun was. She could barely open her eyes against its glare, and the sound that pulsed in her ears was deafening.

She fought to come fully awake, confused but certain she had been dreaming. Then she felt the hard floor beneath her and became aware that the roaring noise was real. She opened her eyes and was dazzled by the intense flame and heat of the propane heater, a jet of fire blasting only a few feet from her face.

Instinctively, she pushed herself into a roll that took her away from the source of heat. She kept her watering eyes closed tightly, her cheek pressed against the cool surface of the floor. Touching her face with tentative fingers, she was relieved to learn she had not been burned despite her proximity to the intense flame. Memory of where she was rushed into her thoughts, followed closely by questions.

How had she reached the living room? The last thing she remembered was being pushing into the basement, the door closing, catching at the rail to keep from falling down the stairs. Then there was nothing. Had she fallen down the stairs and hit her head?

She opened her eyes. A few more tears slipped down her cheeks, but in moments her eyes began to adjust and she could see again. She noticed that her hands and arms were dotted with dark brown specks. She rubbed her thumb over one spot and it flaked away. Dried blood. Was she hurt? How badly?

She got to her feet and stumbled toward the kitchen. The door to the basement was closed, but the bottom panel had been smashed to bits. Splinters of wood and torn bits of hard yellow foam that formed the door's core littered the floor around it.

She must have done that, she realized. She must have found a hammer or an axe or something and beaten on the door until she had broken a hole through. She was amazed by the evidence of her strength and grateful for her freedom.

She took a few hesitant steps, her head pounding violently. She felt slightly woozy, as if she'd had a couple glasses of wine. She fought to clear her head. She had to think. Where was he? Where was the man who'd pushed her down the stairs? Who was he? And where was Muncie? What if the man was still here?

She spotted a screwdriver lying on top of the plywood someone had placed across the kitchen counters to form a work surface. She knew granite counter tops had been special ordered but they hadn't arrived yet. Eagerly she picked up the screwdriver, clutching it in front of her, just a little less afraid. What if she had to use it? Could she? Would it even be an effective weapon? She didn't want to find out. She only wanted to find Muncie and get the hell out of here.

She glanced through the front windows overlooking the lake. Muncie's pickup was right where she'd seen it when she drove up. He had to be here. She looked past the fireplace to the staircase leading to the second floor. The last thing in the world she wanted to do was climb those stairs. She would be completely exposed, and who knew what might be waiting up there? It's all right, she reassured herself, tightening her grip on the handle of the screwdriver. She still had the entire downstairs to explore. No need to go upstairs yet.

Uncomfortably aware that she was staying downstairs out of fear, she began to search methodically from room to room. All the while she held a silent conversation with herself, berating herself for her cowardice. She had checked the utility room near the kitchen and was walking toward the hall to the downstairs bedrooms when the propane heater sputtered and died.

The silence struck like a slap. She could hear her own panting breath, the blood surging with every beat of her heart. She hadn't realized how much she had been counting on the roar of the heater to cover her steps, to mask her movements in case the man who had pushed her was still around. And she had been pushed, hadn't she? She hadn't just imagined it. She wasn't having some sort of psychotic episode or a nervous breakdown. Though if she was, who could blame her? No, she'd been fine for years. She had worked through her problems, accepted her fears, conquered her depression. Besides, she had never imagined things before, not even when she was at her worst. She certainly hadn't imagined Bunny.

Immobilized by the silence, she spotted what she hadn't known she'd been looking for. It was no larger than a dime and almost as perfectly round. It was the color of rust. She had no doubt what it was. She swallowed. The sound of scrub jays and wind rustling the pine branches outside reached her. There was a sudden popping noise, the sort of sound a house makes as it settles. She started.

Wanting not to, but unable to take her eyes away, she looked at the drop of blood on the floor and then, at the periphery of her vision saw another, and when she looked beyond that yet another. She followed the trail of spots, some as small as the first, others wider and more oval in shape. She shook herself out of her unnatural focus on the blood when she came to their end and she found herself facing a closed door at the end of the hallway.

She stood in front of the door for a long moment before she reached for the door knob. It felt cool and smooth in her hand. She could have happily stood there all day and most of the night admiring it, if that meant she would not have to turn it, push the door open.

But she did.

Chapter 18

It was a bedroom. Not large enough for a master bedroom, perhaps meant for children or guests. The floor was covered with canvas drop clothes. The walls were freshly painted in a light shade of mocha, except for where the blood had splashed and run.

Red is his favorite color, she thought inanely. She could see that Muncie was wearing his favorite red flannel shirt, tucked into faded, paint streaked jeans. He was on his back, his booted feet toward her, one knee bent, his face turned toward the wall. His dark hair was matted against the side of his face, held in place by blood, sticky and shining wet.

What she would have done next, screamed or fainted or run she would never know, because at that moment Muncie moaned and moved his legs. She hurried to him, fell to her knees and saw the hammer. It had been dropped beside his hand, as if he had taken it up and swung it and. . .

Ever hear the one about the guy they found with his hands tied behind him and five bullet holes in his back? Suicide, said the coroner. But that couldn't be the punch line. That wasn't even funny. Austin mentally shook herself, afraid of the strange twists her thoughts were taking.

Then Muncie's eyes opened and Austin saw with relief that he was conscious and aware.

"Don't move," she said, "I'm going to find something to stop the bleeding." She ran down the hall to the kitchen and the roll of paper towels she had seen there earlier. She ran back, tearing towels off and wadding them into a pad to hold against the wound.

Sitting up with a groan, Muncie took them from her and held them to his head. Looking past Austin to the doorway he asked, "Where is he?"

"Who?"

"Will."

"He was here?"

"Who else would have done this?"

"You saw him?"

Muncie shook his head. "He must have snuck up on me. I didn't hear him."

"How do you know it was Will?"

Muncie shrugged and closed his eyes, then opened them suddenly. "Did you hear something?"

Austin held her breath and listened. There was – something.

"You need an ambulance. Where's your cell phone?"

"Batteries dead. Forgot to charge it. What about yours?"

"Home on the charger."

"Obviously genetic," Muncie quipped. Austin sighed with relief. If he could make jokes…

"You can drive me to the hospital if you want. Ambulances are for rich folk."

"Are you sure?" Austin asked.

"I'm sure."

She helped Muncie to his feet. He swayed dangerously at first, but then took one slow step after another. Their progress was slower and more awkward because Austin refused to relax her grip on the screwdriver she was still carrying. She left him leaning against the front of the house while she dashed to her truck and brought it around to the door. The brakes squealed as she came to a rocking stop, her driving as erratic as her nerves. With a sense that she was being watched, she helped Muncie into the passenger seat and belted him in. Then she climbed behind the wheel, locked the doors and finally put the screwdriver on the dash.

Conscious of Muncie moaning softly beside her, she did her best to turn the truck without jerky movements and accelerated smoothly away from the house. As they bumped onto the main road, Austin caught a flash of white in the trees.

"Look. Is that a car?" she asked.

"I think I'm going to pass out." Muncie answered.

Austin slammed the gas pedal to the floor. The truck hesitated, then surged forward, picking up speed.

Chapter 19

There were so many questions Austin wanted answered, but Muncie was in no shape to answer them. She'd concentrated on keeping him awake, having heard somewhere that that was important if someone had a head injury. She didn't know if it was true, but she wasn't going to take any chances.

Who had attacked Muncie? Was it Will? She had been so sure he was telling the truth about his father and why he had run from the police. While he told the story she had almost been able to feel his frustration and anger, could see the Mercedes slide lazily down the hill. But there were pathological liars, people who lied so convincingly even they believed it. Maybe he was one of those. How would she know? Had she put Muncie in danger by not turning Will in when she had the chance?

The only thing she'd done since arriving at the hospital, aside from pacing, was to call Janice. Now, hearing the quick tap of hurried steps, she looked up to see Janice hurrying across the waiting room toward her.

"Austin, what happened? Is he ok?" She looked as

upset as Austin felt.

"They say it's a concussion, maybe not so bad. They said they'd come tell me more soon."

"What happened?" Janice said, repeating herself.

Austin led Janice to a quiet corner of the waiting room and they both sat down. Taking a deep breath Austin said, "Someone attacked him from behind. They hit him in the head, with – with a hammer. He was working at the Lake House, in one of the bedrooms and he says the next thing he knew he was on his knees. He doesn't even remember getting hit the first time. He says all he remembers is being on his knees and then the person hitting him again, only it missed his head and hit his shoulder. He went down anyway and must have been hit again because he blacked out."

"My God, that's horrible. First Bunny, now Muncie. Why is this happening?"

"I don't know," Austin said quietly. She shut her eyes for a moment, rubbed her temples. Then she opened her eyes and, looking at Janice, said hesitantly., "I need to tell you about Will." She told the story of Will's appearance at the store and her idea of getting him to turn himself in to the police.

"So maybe what I did was let a murderer into my house. Maybe he was after me but he got scared when Muncie drove up. Could that be what set him after Muncie? Did he get scared and did that make him mad enough so that he tracked Muncie down, found him at The Lake House, and he tried to bash in his head with a hammer? "Is it my fault that Muncie got attacked? I hired Will in the first place. Maybe it's my fault that Bunny's dead too."

"But you were so sure it couldn't be Will," said Janice. "And even if it was him, that doesn't make it your fault.

Please Austin, don't take this on yourself. You did not kill Bunny or do anything wrong. You did not hurt your brother." Janice patted Austin's arm. "Let's sit down. Have you had anything to eat or drink today?"

Austin shook her head. "I'm fine. I don't want anything."

Ignoring her, Janice strode away, only to return a short while later with two steaming cups of hot chocolate. Austin took a sip and nodded her gratitude. She and Janice sat down to wait.

Janice continued to try to convince Austin that she was not to blame for Muncie's injuries.

"We don't even know for sure that it was Will," she argued. "We don't know why Bunny was killed or why Muncie was attacked. How do we know they are even connected?"

"They have to be. It's not like this is some crime-ridden city. This is our quiet little town. When was our last homicide? Five years ago? And that was a stranger, right?"

"That's right. The first summer you spent in Spruce. I remember because my folks were worried you'd get the wrong impression."

"She was a clerk at some store, like Bunny?"

"I think so. Hey, what are you thinking? The police decided it was a hobo. Someone who came into town, took her out near the train yards and killed her."

"Crushed her skull with a metal pipe, is what they said."

"Don't remind me," said Janice with a shudder.

"Did I tell you the police discovered Bunny had been beaten over the head and knocked unconscious, maybe was already dead before she was stabbed with the trowel?"

Austin asked.

"I didn't, but you're starting to creep me out."

"I wonder how strong a person would have to be to kill someone that way?"

"Okay, that's enough. I think you should leave all this speculation to the . . ."

"Austin Ward?" A nurse called from the doorway leading to the emergency room. Austin and Janice followed her to the nurses' station where a doctor joined them.

"Your brother is going to be fine," he reassured Austin . "As we expected, the x-rays show no sign of a fracture. We are assuming he sustained only a mild concussion. We want to keep him overnight, just for observation. However, I'm fairly sure we'll be able to release him in the morning."

"Can I, can we, see him?" asked Austin.

"The police are talking to him right now, and he's filling out a report, but you can go back if you like. They will probably want to speak with you as well. The nurse will show you the way."

The sharp medicinal smell so specific to hospitals was strong, triggering Austin's memory of that night she'd arrived to see her mother one last time, only to learn she was too late. She fought the urge to turn and leave, and instead meekly followed Janice and the nurse into the back. They walked quietly past rows of curtained rooms, each with its own gurney and baffling array of lifesaving equipment until they reached Muncie's.

Muncie was sitting on the edge of a gurney, his feet dangling, a white gauze bandage wrapped around his head. He was speaking softly to two police officers, one who seemed to be asking questions, the other scribbling notes on a small notepad. Muncie introduced Austin and Janice to the officers and immediately the officers asked Austin to step into the hall with them. Janice stayed behind with Muncie.

"Do you think the attack on your brother is related to the attack on Naomi? Why did you go to The Lake House? Were your brother and Naomi involved?"

The officer's questions came fast, and though she tried to answer them as thoroughly as possible, they did not seem happy with her answers. She was beginning to lose her temper, and was close to bursting out with something rude about why they weren't out looking for the killer, when she heard a familiar voice.

"Excuse me."

She turned to see Blake striding toward her. He swept up and protectively put his arm around her shoulders. "You all right?"

She nodded. Blake finally acknowledged the presence of the two policemen. "Ms. Ward has had a real rough day. I'm taking her home. If you want to talk to her, call her lawyer. You have a lawyer, don't you, Austin.?"

"No," she said, "I don't."

"That's okay. We'll get you one. Ms. Ward's attorney will be contacting your department. Now, if you'll excuse us." He gently steered Austin away, and before she knew it they were passing through the front door of the hospital.

"That was impressive," she said once she was safely seated inside his rental car. "But I have to let Muncie know what's going on and my friend, Janice, is still in there. I left my stupid phone on the charger."

Blake handed her his cell phone. From the calm of Blake's car she called Janice.

"Blake showed up while the police were asking me about what happened. He sort of dragged me out of there. I really don't want to deal with any more questions right now. Do you think. . ."

"Of course I'll stay with Muncie," Janice said, without waiting for Austin to finish. "I'll stay until he's settled in a room and then call you at home."

"Thank you so much, Janice."

"Don't thank me, just go home and get some rest."

"I am. Quit nagging."

"Right, that's going to happen," Janice said, and hung up.

Austin handed Blake his phone and said, "Thank you for the rescue."

"That's me," he replied, "the white knight. May I drive the lady home?"

"I have my truck."

"But you look like you shouldn't be driving it."

"Don't be silly. I drove Muncie to the hospital, didn't I?"

"That's different. You were running on adrenaline then. I bet you're exhausted. Yes?"

Austin nodded. "I'm a little shaky, yes."

"Then don't argue.

"I don't think I have the energy to argue."

"Good."

"Blake?"

"Yeah," he asked, as he started the car.

"Why were you at the hospital? How did you know I was there?"

"I didn't know. I was there to visit someone."

"But I thought you didn't know anyone around here."

"You and my real estate gal are about it, that's true. She fell off her horse and broke her leg this morning. She left me a message because we had an appointment today, so I thought I'd drop in, get her some flowers, tell her not to worry about anything. You know."

"That's so sweet."

"Sweet? Well, that's not exactly how I'd put it. Just wanted to make sure she didn't need anything."

"Did you even get a chance to see her?"

"No, but that's okay. They don't keep you in the hospital long for a break, you know. She might have already checked out. Anyway, I'm just glad I was there to get those cops off you. Not real clear on what was going on back there, but I could see you weren't happy about it. Guess you'll tell me about it someday, when you feel like it."

"Oh, I'm sorry. I wasn't trying to hide anything." Austin then filled Blake in on what had happened in her life since the last time that she'd seen him. She told him about Bunny's murder and the attack on Muncie and even a little about Muncie's suspicions about Will. By the time they pulled up to her house he was as up-to-date on what was going on as she was and as puzzled.

They were still discussing it as they got out of his car, and it seemed perfectly natural that Blake should walk her to the door and that she would invite him in for a cup of coffee.

As they stepped over the threshold and Austin switched on the lights, she realized she was happy that Blake was there. She did not want to be alone. Night would come soon. Host of the darkness and of her fear, and she could not face it, not just yet.

"Got anything to drink?" Blake asked. "I think we could both use a shot of something."

Austin agreed. "Beer? Tequila?"

"Yes, those sound about right."

Austin laughed and shrugging off her coat, walked into the kitchen to get both. "Just hang your coat right there, by the door," she said, gesturing to the coat rack.

"I have to warn you this Tequila's pretty old," she said. "I think it was left over from a Fourth of July barbecue."

"I promise not to complain," he said.

Austin placed two shot glasses and the bottle of tequila on the counter that divided the kitchen from the dining room. Blake carried them to the dining room table and Austin took two cold beers from the refrigerator and joined him.

"Any luck with the property search?" she asked, after she'd taken a seat.

"Don't you want to talk about your brother and all the things that have been going on?"

"No. I absolutely do not want to talk about it, or think about it. I appreciate your talking to me about all this on the way here, but right now I just want to forget, for a little while."

He lifted one of the shot glasses. "In that case..."

Austin picked up her drink as well. They clinked glasses and emptied them. Blake smiled as Austin gasped and took a big pull of beer to ease the burn in her throat.

"You were right, that is some nasty stuff," he said. He refilled their glasses but didn't drink again. Instead, he reached across the table and put his hand on top of

Austin's. His long fingers stroked the back of her hand. She could not meet his eyes. She watched as his fingers slid up the back of her hand to her wrist and then traveled slowly up her arm, barely touching the cotton fabric of her blouse but sending goose bumps across her skin. She hadn't been touched in so long. She knew she should probably pull away, say something amusing, turn it into a joke. She barely knew him. She closed her eyes.

His response was to stand up and move behind her. She felt his hands rest on her shoulders and then they were sliding down her arms, his touch firmer this time. She kept her eyes closed as his hands slid back up to her shoulders, resting there, his fingers touching the bare skin above her collarbone. Then his hands slid across the front of her blouse and his fingers fumbled with the top button.

Her eyes snapped open and she sat bolt upright.

"Wait," she demanded. "Stop." She practically jumped to her feet, almost upsetting her chair and he backed up a step. She swung around to face him.

"I'm sorry. I didn't mean for . . ." She began to explain, to apologize.

He reached up and his hand was in her hair, tangled in it, pulling her forward. He took a step, pressing himself against her. She could smell the sharp tang of tequila on his breath. She jerked free. Red-faced and determined she pushed him away.

"Stop it."

"Stop what? I haven't done anything," he said. "Yet."

He reached for her again and this time he kissed her, or at least tried to. His lips were on her mouth and his hands around her waist but she turned her head quickly to the side and struggled to break free.

Austin felt trapped, her breath came fast, shallow panting breaths that weren't enough to fill her lungs. She would have fallen to her knees, too weak to stand, if Blake hadn't been holding her.

The doorbell rang.

Blake let her go.

The moment she was free, strength flowed back into her body. She stumbled away from Blake and toward the door, toward rescue.

Blake stopped her. He put his hand on her arm and pulled her around.

"I don't know what that was that just happened. I don't know why you got so scared, but I didn't do a thing to you. You remember that. I didn't do a thing."

Austin looked down at the fingers wrapped around her upper arm and Blake released his hold.

"Austin, honest I'm sorry. I got carried away." Blake's tone had changed from angry to conciliatory in an instant. "Please Austin. I wouldn't have done anything you didn't want."

The doorbell rang again.

"It's okay," Austin lied, annoyed by the quiver in her voice. She pushed her fingers through her hair, tugged down the front of her blouse. "We'll talk about it later. Maybe I overreacted. I can get freaked out when someone holds me too tight, like I can't breathe, you know?"

Blake nodded, though Austin could tell it was less an agreement with what she was saying, than an acknowledgment that whatever had happened between them was over.

"I'd better get the door," Austin said.

Blake nodded, looking somewhat dazed. She imagined she wore a similar expression.

Austin paused at the door to run her fingers through her hair again and then opened it. Mark was standing there. His hand raised to knock on the door. Surprised to see her therapist, she didn't know what to say.

"Austin. Sorry. I know you weren't expecting me," he explained. "Your friend Janice Simmons called me this afternoon. She left a message that your brother had been hurt and that you might want to see me. If this is a bad time, I'd be happy to leave."

"No, this isn't a bad time. Please come in." Austin opened the door and stepped aside.

"Thank you," he said, stepping across the threshold. Then, seeing Blake, he stopped.

Austin stepped into the living room. "Mark, this is my friend Blake, um Blake?"

"Roberts," Blake supplied, stepping forward to shake Mark's hand.

"Mark is helping me." Austin said without explaining further. "He's here to talk to me about Muncie."

"Cop?" Blake snapped, with what Austin thought was a bit too much hostility.

"No," said Austin. "Just a friend."

"I see. Well I was just leaving. Austin, can I call you later?"

"Of course."

"All right then. I'll talk to you soon. I'm sorry. . ."

"Don't be sorry. We'll work it out later."

He leaned down and gave her a light kiss on the cheek, then took his coat and left. Austin shut the door behind him."

"Sorry for the interruption," Mark said.

"You aren't interrupting," Austin reassured him. Blake really was just leaving. He drove me home from the hospital because I was too upset to drive."

Austin suddenly realized that the top of her blouse was gaping and felt a blush blaze across her face. To hide it she turned away. "Let me tidy up a bit and I'll be right there. Just take a seat anywhere. Oh, and you can hang your coat up there by the door if you like."

Mark looked around the living room, with its old wood plank floors and river-rock fireplace, and chose a comfortable chair, placed to catch the warm slant of afternoon sunlight streaming through the big picture window.

"I like your house," he said as Austin returned.

"It's old and sort of beat up."

"But comfortable and sort of friendly," he offered.

"Yeah, I think so too," Austin agreed. She had buttoned her blouse, run a comb through her hair and made faces at herself in the mirror.

"Would you like something to drink? Beer? Soda?"

"Icewater would be great."

"Okay."

Austin grabbed the tequila, beer bottles, and glasses and put them in the kitchen. Then she filled a glass with ice and water and grabbed a can of soda for herself. She handed Mark his water and sat on the end of the couch, her legs curled beneath her comfortably, as they talked.

"You said your friend drove you home because you were too upset to drive?" he asked.

"That's right."

"And were you?"

"What?"

"Were you too upset to drive?"

"I think I would have managed. Janice worries too much."

She placed her soda on the end table and crossed her arms. "Everyone worries about me too much. Who we should be worrying about is Muncie."

"Tell me about it."

Austin did. She started with being pushed into the basement and her escape. Then she talked about finding Muncie and thinking he was dead and later her fear that he might die on the way to the hospital.

"I've never been so afraid in my life. I know that sounds funny, given that I'm afraid so often. But it's different. When I find myself in darkness that's a special kind of scary. I have these, what my family used to call "episodes." The fear reaches a certain point, and I just shut down, black out, and later I don't remember anything. With Muncie I was scared too, but I couldn't just "go away." I had to drive. I had to take care of him. You understand?"

"I think so. In this case the fear was more enabling then crippling."

"I suppose you could put it that way. It gave me more energy or courage or something. You should have seen me helping Muncie to the truck. I was so angry and scared at the same time. Here I am with this skinny little screwdriver but just determined I'd use it on anyone who got in the way." Austin smiled at the image this conjured.

"It's been pretty awful for you lately," Mark said, making it a statement.

"Yeah, pretty damn awful. First Bunny and now Muncie. What happened to them has to be tied together somehow, but I just don't see it. Why would anyone want to hurt them? What could they possibly have in common?"

"Well, I can think of one thing. You."

"Me?"

"I've been thinking about it. You told me you were locked in the potting shed. How do you know the attacker didn't mean to kill you? How do you know Muncie didn't scare him away before he had the chance? What about the attack on Bunny? Could that have been a case of mistaken identity?"

"But why Muncie? Surely he couldn't be mistaken for me."

"No, but you told me it was Muncie who found you in the shed and got you out. What if the killer was frustrated that Muncie got in the way? What if it was retribution for his interference?"

"That's a lot of "what ifs", but it sort of makes sense. At least as much sense as any other theory I've heard. God, it's such a nightmare," Austin proclaimed. "I'm beginning to get spooked."

"Well I could be completely wrong. In fact, I'm probably way off. I just wanted to throw the idea out there, as crazy as it might be. I just want you to consider everything and be careful."

"I'll be careful, believe me. I'm too nervous not to be careful. I wish I had a dog. A nice big Rottweiler would do, or maybe a Doberman. I hear they always go for the throat. I would really appreciate a dog like that right now."

"Well, I can't help you there," Mark said with a grin. "I'm not packing a Rottweiler, but I would be willing to stay here tonight, if it would make you feel safer."

"You have got to be the world's best therapist," Austin enthused, an edge of nervousness tightening her throat. "Are you this way with all your patients?"

"No, but not all my patients have a couch as comfortable as yours looks, and most aren't dealing with a homicidal maniac. And most importantly, I just bought a boat, and if something happens to you, how will I make the payments?"

"Now that last thing sounds like a valid reason to me," agreed Austin, "but I'm still going to turn you down. I have a good support system. My friend Janice can spend the night if I get the willies, and a couple of the guys from my landscaping crew live just minutes away. I'll be fine."

"I guess you will be. You're pretty resilient from what I've seen so far."

"Plus, I've got your number."

"And I want you to use it. If you are feeling anxious or if anything else happens, or even if you just need to talk, I want you to promise you'll call."

"I promise," Austin agreed. She had been a little anxious about his offer to stay. No doubt a side effect of her struggle with Blake. But Mark's pointed comment about her couch had reassured her that there was no hidden purpose behind his offer to spend the night.

"Well, then, I guess I'll get out of here. Let you get some rest. We'll talk more in a couple days. You're still planning to keep your appointment, aren't you?"

"Are you kidding? How else are you going to make those boat payments? I can tell you from experience that the bank is not your friend. They are not going to wait for you to find someone even more unstable."

"I appreciate your advice," said Mark, a smile lighting up his dark brown eyes.

"Well why not, it's free," Austin joked playfully. "I'll see you soon."

"It's a date."

As Austin watched Mark's jeep drive away, she remembered how exhausted she was. Too tired to even walk to her bedroom, she stretched out on the couch, pulled one of her mom's hand-knit Afghans over her, and in moments was deeply asleep.

Chapter 20

Austin woke, completely disoriented by her nap. Her body seemed unhappy to find that instead of morning, it was late evening. She still felt tired and achy, as if she were coming down with the flu.

She hoped her nap wasn't going to set off a round of insomnia. In college she'd thrown off her sense of time on several occasions, pulling all night study marathons. Nights of insomnia had usually been the price.

Austin made a quick call to the hospital to find that Muncie was doing well but was asleep. Deciding she didn't want to spend the rest of the night in a sleepy haze, she took a quick shower, brushed her teeth, and changed into pajamas.

While she performed these mundane tasks, her mind raced from one concern to another. Her first thought was that she had to find a way to get her truck from the hospital parking lot where she'd left it. She regretted having let Blake drive her home. Not only was she going to have to deal with the truck, but also there was that whole unpleasant scene with him. As she remembered, her feelings ranged back and forth, from righteous indignation to abject shame to guilt. The emotional overload made her nerves sizzle. As she brushed her hair she noticed her hands were trembling. If she could just find a resolution, know what was right.

Would Blake have stopped if Mark hadn't rang the doorbell? Had she overreacted? She had invited him in after all. She had encouraged him, at least she hadn't discouraged him, not at first. How much had her phobia of being constrained, locked in, added to her reaction? And the most haunting thought of all, now that she was safe: had she just blown the possibility of the best relationship of her life?

This had been a horrible day, she decided. She counted off the reasons. One, Muncie had been attacked. Two, she had almost slept with, and then had to fight off Blake, a virtual stranger. God, half the time she couldn't even remember his last name. Three, she had discovered she was starting to like Mark, maybe a little too much. She made a face at herself in the mirror. Falling for her therapist. Just like every other lonely female on the planet. "Now isn't that just typical," she said, scolding her image. And four, she had no idea what to do about numbers 1 through 3.

But Muncie was going to be fine, she reminded herself. At least that had turned out better than it might have. Blake was pretty secondary to that. She'd talk to him, on the phone at first, see how it went and whether she wanted see him again. Liking Mark wasn't even really a problem, just something to be aware of. By the time she was finished with her nightly routine she had talked herself out of most of her anxiety and was suddenly hungry.

Knowing she wouldn't be ready for bed for some time she switched on the television on her way to the kitchen. She'd make something nice and hot to eat, have some tea, take care of herself. By morning, everything would look better.

Chapter 21

In the morning Austin called the hospital and learned that Muncie had already been discharged. Relieved on one hand but annoyed that he hadn't called, she tried his cell phone. Instead of ringing she went right into voice mail, so she suspected he hadn't got around to charging it yet. She left a message for him to call her back, hung up, and called a cab.

The cab dropped her off beside her pickup and she climbed in and drove straight to Muncie's apartment. As she pulled into one of the guest slots she noticed a familiar blue Honda pulling out of her brother's parking space. Before she could wave, Janice had turned onto the main street.

She knocked on Muncie's door, and when he opened it she was surprised to see that he looked as if nothing had ever happened. He was wearing a black T-shirt tucked into his usual washed out jeans and was barefoot. In his free hand he held a cup of coffee. His dark, reddish-brown hair was brushed neatly back out of his eyes and his smile was wide and immediate when he saw her.

"Hey, it's my hero," he said. "Come in."

"You look great," she said. "Where's your bandage."

"Took it off once the bleeding stopped. Nothing to see but a couple stitches in the melon." He lifted a section of hair and Austin winced at the sight of a shaved patch of skin and a trio of stitches.

"That's pretty."

"I bet. I still have a headache too, but hell, I'm alive. It's sort of like coming out of a bad bout of the flu. You still feel a little crappy, but you know you're getting better and the whole world looks good."

"I know what you mean", she said, remembering a similar feeling after her nap the night before.

"Coffee?" He asked, moving through his small studio toward the kitchenette.

"Of course," said Austin.

"This is a special blend I picked up in Portland. You're gonna love it."

Muncie's apartment was small but neat. The kitchenette, basically a wall containing a mini fridge, two burner stove and oven, small sink and about three feet of counter space was to the right. He took a cup from a row of hooks under a cabinet and began to fill it with dark, rich coffee. The scent of it filled the air.

Austin sat at the glass-topped table that had been designed, along with the ornate metal chairs, to be lawn furniture, but served as Muncie's dining set. She glanced around the apartment casually, taking in the sparse furniture. There was a futon couch covered in dark blue, unfolded into a bed and covered with a blue and white quilt. A whitewashed entertainment center held a small television and a stereo system. A corner desk, also whitewashed, held a computer and a row of neatly aligned books and disks. Two orange buckets contained rolls of blueprints. The only thing out of place was a single coffee cup sitting in the sink.

"So," she asked. "Was that Janice I passed on my way in?"

Without hesitation Muncie said, "Sure was. When she was leaving last night she offered to pick me up and bring me home this morning. Since she lives in town it seemed better than making you drive all the way out."

"Oh." Austin said, unable to keep all traces of disappointment from her voice.

"Hoping for a big fat secret? An affair maybe?" Muncie asked, handing her a steaming mug of coffee.

"Wouldn't surprise me," Austin admitted, taking a tentative sip of the coffee and then nodding her approval.

"Thought you'd like it. Why wouldn't it surprise you?"

"You've always liked Janice, and she used to have a little crush on you in college."

"She did?"

"Well, she thought you were cute anyway."

"Cute. Great. That's what every guy wants to hear. That he's cute."

"Handsome?"

"Too late. So what's up?"

"Nothing's up. I called the hospital and they told me you'd been discharged. I couldn't reach you. By the way, charge your damn cell phone, will you?"

He gestured to the counter where his cell phone sat in its charging unit.

"Well, good. Anyway, I left my truck in town last night

and since I had to come get it anyway, I thought I'd see how you were feeling. I know you're hard-headed, but no one's *that* hard-headed."

Her playful tone was at odds with the chill that swept through Austin at the memory of Muncie lying at her feet, blood soaking his hair. She put the coffee on the counter and rubbed her arms, but the chill went deep. It made goose flesh on her arms and made her bones feel like they were clanking under her skin, like icicles.

"You okay?" Muncie asked.

"Yeah, didn't sleep well, that's all. So, what are you doing today?"

"I have to go to the police station this morning. They want to know if I remember anything else. Also, they're sending an escort out with me to The Lake House, just to do some kind of safety check. Take a look around, you know."

"That's good. It makes me feel better about you going out there. Actually, part of the reason I came over this morning was to ask you not to go there by yourself. But I guess I don't have to worry."

"Nope. Until they catch Will I'm playing it safe."

Austin bit back the reply that leapt to mind. She knew it would do no good to try to convince Muncie to give Will the benefit of the doubt. When it came to Will's guilt, Muncie had no doubts whatsoever.

"You know," Muncie said, "I hate to bring this up but you were attacked at the house too."

Austin picked up her coffee and leaned against the counter. "I don't know that I'd call it an attack," she mused. "It was more like he was getting me out of the way, so he could go after you, or hide what he'd done to you. I'm not sure about the order of things. He didn't try to hurt me and he couldn't have known about how being in a dark basement would affect me."

"Maybe," Muncie agreed reluctantly. "It's sure a damn puzzle."

"Yeah, I keep wondering why I wasn't hurt," Austin agreed. "He didn't hurt me, and somehow I didn't hurt myself. If you saw how much damage I did to that door — you'd think I'd at least have a splinter or something."

"Or a broken nail," Muncie teased.

"You'd think," Austin said, smiling at her big brother.

"Then you'd really be pissed."

"Absolutely."

"You still so sure Will is innocent?" Muncie asked, taking Austin by surprise.

"I never said I was sure. I just thought we shouldn't jump to conclusions about his guilt," she replied. "You said you didn't see him at The Lake House. Are you sure?"

"Yes. I mean–I don't know. How about you? Do you remember anything else about getting pushed into the basement, or after?"

"Nothing clearly. I sort of have this sense that the guy was stronger, stockier than Will. You know Will is tall but pretty slender."

"Yeah, but you were scared, that could have made him seem bigger. Hell, how do we know he wasn't a she?"

"I suppose," Austin sighed. She finished the last of her coffee and rinsed the mug, then set it in the sink next to its mate. "Next time you go to Portland, tell me and I'll give you some money so you can pick up some of that for me."

"I thought you'd like it. But it might be some time

before I get back to Portland. I'm not so sure I'm going to move back there. College? Come on. I'm too old."

"You're thirty," corrected Austin. "That's not old. Besides, it's a commuter college, half the students will be older than you are, and even if they aren't, it didn't seem to bother you before. What's the real reason you don't want to go?"

"Money?"

"Dad left you just as much as he left me, and from what I can tell you haven't touched a penny."

"Well then, I guess I don't know the reason."

"Well I do. You have some dumb idea that you have to hang around and hold my hand. I appreciate that you've helped me when I've needed it. I admit I've had a few rough times, but I'm better now and I need for you to see that, and to believe it."

"I do see it. You are doing great, just great," he said facetiously. "One of your employees was just murdered. I found you unconscious not too long ago, and I know under your makeup you still have what was a pretty nasty black eye. Yep, you're doing great."

"Ok, point taken, but you have to admit I'm handling all that pretty well. Haven't even thought once about opening a vein."

"That's not funny. Don't joke about that."

"Ok. Ok," Austin promised. Then she said, "I have to run. I have a lot of errands to take care of."

"Sure."

"And we'll talk about this college thing some more soon."

"If we have to."

"We do." Austin drew up the collar of her coat and stepped into the bright blue morning, shutting the door behind her.

Her next stop would be Bunny's parents' home. She dreaded the thought, but knew she had to do it.

She pulled into the driveway of the ranch-style home on a quiet street in the suburbs. Its bright yellow walls and white trim was cheerful, its windows were gleaming, the lawn was well-maintained, with neatly edged flower beds and a row of rose bushes, their roots heavily mulched against the killing temperatures to come.

She knocked on the door, waited, then rang the bell. There was no answer and no cars in the driveway, though that didn't mean much. The family cars could have been inside the garage.

After knocking one more time, Austin turned to go back to her truck and saw a middle-aged woman, with bright red hair and a jarringly purple sweater, hurrying toward her.

"Are you here to mow the lawn?" she asked, shooting a glance at Austin's truck and the sign on the door that read "Blue Spruce Landscaping" in large letters and in smaller script her phone and license numbers.

"The Ames aren't here. Maybe you didn't hear about their daughter?"

"Yes, I heard."

"Well then I guess you didn't hear that they sent her body to the family burial plot in Maryland. Can you imagine that, sending her all the way to Maryland, a girl who was born and raised right here. Why, what in the world is she going to do there? Well, I suppose it doesn't matter now, does it?" The strange woman rushed on, barely pausing for air. "They took it hard, you know. She was their third girl; the baby. They spoiled her, of course. Let her do any damn thing she wanted. She had nice brown hair one day and the next that white blonde. It was shocking. Then the next thing you know she's moved away, got her own place, with who, that's what I wonder?"

"Do you know when they'll be coming back?" Austin interrupted.

"Not a clue. But then they aren't that friendly you know. Keep to themselves, mostly. Religious of course, regular worship group meets here every Saturday. Not sure what religion that would be, meeting on Saturday, but there you are."

Austin found herself backing away and moving around her truck to escape the nasty, gossipy neighbor.

"Kind of late to be mowing. Going to be snowing soon."

"Yes, I suppose you're right. Well, thank you." Austin climbed into her truck and slammed the door. The woman, who had followed Austin step for step to the driver's side appeared to be waiting for Austin to do the polite thing and roll the window down. Instead Austin started the pickup and threw it into reverse, practically squealing her tires in her desire to get away.

As she drove home, the realization that Bunny had finally gotten her wish and escaped Spruce only added to the sense of loss. Austin hoped that the memory of Bunny's open smile, her distinctive white-blond hair and the mischievous glint in her wide blue eyes would haunt her forever. As long as she was not forgotten, in a way, Bunny would still be there.

Chapter 22

Austin spent a restless night and in the morning called Muncie.

"Is this going to be a daily thing?" he asked, once he realized who it was.

"I'm just worried about you."

"You saw me yesterday. Nothing much has changed, honest."

"You said you were going out to the house," Austin said.

"I did. I went in a patrol car. It was sort of cool. They checked everything out. They had already been there earlier so it was more just asking me things, where did stuff happen? What did I remember?"

"So it went OK?"

"Sure."

"So why aren't you at work?"

"Because I have a tiny headache. Not a tumor. Not a brain bleed. Just a headache. But I decided it would be a good idea to take one more day off."

"Good."

"Is it?" he asked.

"Yes, at least this way I have an idea where you are."

"Control freak. What are you doing today?"

"I don't know," said Austin. "Pick up some groceries. I have an appointment with my therapist in a little while."

"That's good, right?"

"Yeah," she said awkwardly, "It seems to be. Well, if you're really okay."

"I am really okay," he reassured her, not keeping the exasperation out of his voice. "Now would you go already, you're interfering with "Days of Our Lives.".

"I had no idea," she said, trying to sound serious but unable to keep a smile out of her voice as she thought of her brother watching soap operas.

At one o'clock that afternoon she stepped into Mark's office and sat in the brown chair just as she had the last two times, but this time she wasn't nearly as nervous. She felt comfortable here now, she realized, in this chair and with Mark.

She rarely felt easy with new people so quickly. Of course, the nature of therapy, talking openly with someone, was bound to cut through some of the usual social meandering, but she'd seen therapists before. This seemed different.

She tried to analyze how Mark made her feel. In some way he seemed as close as her brother. No, she decided, that wasn't quite right. It was more as if he were an old lover, someone she'd had a long and intense affair with, shared an unusual intimacy with, so that even though the affair ended what was left was a mutual respect, a type of caring. If I believed in reincarnation, she thought to herself,

I'd almost think we'd known each other in a past life. Or maybe I'm really just attracted to him and don't know how to deal with it, so I'm making up stories in my head.

Just the sight of Mark's green and gray Columbia jacket, tossed carelessly over the back of the monstrous coach, filled her with a sense of warmth. It was hard to deny that, whether or not they'd shared a past life, she was definitely affected by him in this one.

When Mark sat down, she smiled at him sheepishly, glad he couldn't read her mind. She dug through her purse for the insurance forms he'd given her at their first meeting. He took them from her, tucking them between the pages of the yellow legal pad on his lap.

"Tough week," he said emphatically.

"Understatement," she said, agreeing.

He nodded, waiting for her to continue.

"The police called," she finally said. "Know what they told me? They wanted to know where we all were last Sunday night. I thought Bunny was killed on Monday but it turns out I was wrong. It was Sunday night. She was out there for two whole days. I was there. Did I tell you? I was there on Monday. I had to check on something, and I hung around and made some calls. All that time Bunny was out there, like that, in the potting shed. It makes me sick when I think about it."

"There was nothing you could have done for her."

"I know, and it isn't going to make me go off the deep end or anything. But still, it bothers me. And there's something else."

"Yes?"

"I have to go back. To the start of it. To the beginning."

"Please," he urged.

"I told you about the bomb shelter, remember?"

"Who could forget?"

"I wasn't lying when I said I don't remember getting locked in. All my memories are really my family's memories. Memories of a story they told me. They said after the boys closed the bomb shelter door they couldn't get it open. Eventually they told my mother, but she couldn't open it either. She managed to flag down some MPs, and finally they managed to pry it open.

"They found me in a state of shock. At first they even thought I was dead. My respirations were slow, my skin glossy and pale. There was blood all over my hands from where I'd torn my nails trying to get the door open, and a big bruise on my forehead where they think I rammed my head into the door. They thought maybe I'd concussed myself and had brain damage. They took me to the hospital and injected me with something that brought me out of it. I was fine then. No memories, but fine."

"No physical damage?"

"Nothing they could find. Mentally? Emotionally? I don't know. How can you measure? They said I was maybe a little quieter than I had been, but kids change, you know?"

Abruptly, Austin got to the point. "Do you believe in evil?" she asked. "I mean real evil. Not just people who do thoughtlessly cruel things, or crazy people who have no empathy, but evil as an entity, a spirit, if you wish. Something that can reach out and interact with us. Do you believe in that sort of evil?"

Mark took a moment to consider. "I don't think so. I think most of that comes out of our superstitions, things that we can't explain any other way. Hurricanes, floods, fires, people have often blamed natural disasters on evil. Is that what you mean?"

"I don't know. I guess lately, with everything that's been going on, I've been thinking a lot about good and evil."

"Yes?"

"They say when I came out of it I insisted that someone, or something, was in the bomb shelter with me, that I could hear breathing. They explained it away as an echo. But what if they were wrong? What if there was something there? It was a bomb shelter after all, built to serve a purpose that everyone was terrified of. Think of the fear that generation was forced to live with. They had the Cuban missile crisis, their kids being put through those awful drills, the defense books and the sirens. Couldn't all that terror come together and form some sort of – thing?"

"Thing?"

"Or entity, or shadow or some dark presence, something in the dark?"

"It sounds very Stephen King, Dean Koontz to me."

"I know, or like The Outer Limits. Ooooh eeee ohhhh."Austin tried unsuccessfully to imitate the show's theme music.

Mark grinned and asked, "Is there a reason that you're wondering about this?"

"I don't know. No, I guess not really. It's just easier to think that there's some sort of curse or something evil that has decided to poke around in my life. I guess I'm looking for a reason when there may not be one. I suppose you think my concerns about an old evil are just a way of expressing my current fears?"

"Hey, no self-diagnosis," Mark joked. "I'm the therapist, remember?"

Chapter 23

After much debate, Austin checked in on Muncie one more time. When his voicemail picked up, immediately she hung up. He had probably left his phone off for a reason. No doubt he was taking the rest of the day to relax. Maybe she should do the same.

She opened her front door just as the phone began to ring and managed to get to it before the answering machine took over.

"Hello."

"Hello. Austin?"

"Yes."

"It's Blake."

Austin's stomach dropped.

"Austin?"

"I'm here, sorry."

"Have you got any dinner plans?" he asked.

"No, I hadn't thought about it."

"Have dinner with me."

"I really don't feel like going out. Besides, I just had lunch."

"We can make it whatever time you like. We need to talk."

"I don't know."

"Listen, I'm really sorry about what happened. It will never happen again, I promise. I was stupid. I thought…well I obviously misread what you wanted. Please. Let's just get something to eat and talk. Just talk," he promised.

"I don't know. I really just planned to stay home tonight."

"So how about me coming out there?"

Austin knew if he did that, she was in trouble. Her emotions were shredded. She was feeling too lonely and vulnerable. What if she surrendered to her desire to have a warm body in her bed by encouraging Blake, who she didn't really trust. She wasn't in the habit of picking up strangers, no matter how much she and Janice joked about such things.

"No. You're right," she gave in. "I have to eat anyway. Company would be nice. Why don't you meet me at the Blue Dolphin around six thirty. We'll have a quick dinner and talk. Does that sound okay?"

"Sounds perfect. I'll see you there in an hour."

"Good." She hung up and took a deep breath. Damn. What had she gotten herself into? Well, maybe she did owe him a second chance. She had acted like a tease, inviting him in, letting him touch her. Maybe she had earned some guilt, and going out, when all she really wanted was a nice warm bed and a book to read, was a penance of sorts.

It would also give her the chance to explain that she didn't believe in one-night stands, though given those first few minutes at the table that might be a tough sell.

Having made up her mind to give Blake a second chance, Austin began to think of their dinner as a date. For a while she distracted herself with housework and a crossword puzzle, but finally she had to get ready.

She showered and changed from her jeans and white linen work shirt into a long black suede skirt, knee-high boots, and an emerald green turtleneck. She let her hair down and brushed it out. It fell in loose waves to the middle of her back. She put on a touch of blush, lined her eyes with a kohl pencil, and began to get nervous. As she leaned into the mirror to put on lipstick she felt butterflies fluttering in her stomach and noticed that her hands were trembling, just like the first time she'd gone out with Blake.

She smiled at her image in the mirror. "What is this, high school? Grow up." She made a face at herself.

She expected to find Blake sitting at a table or booth but he was standing outside the diner leaning, as if posed, against the wall near the door. He couldn't have dressed more to her liking if he had been handed a script. He wore a black cowboy hat, skin-tight jeans, and black boots. He had on a denim sheep's wool-lined jacket and a fleece muffler wrapped loosely around his neck. He looked every inch a cowboy dressed up for town. She'd had a thing about cowboys since she'd read her first Zane Grey. But the cowboys she'd met since mostly wore dirty caps with tractor or feed store insignias, chewed and spit tobacco, and smelled like sweat and cows. She had yet to meet one who lived up to their full-blown, media-fed fantasy, until now.

She looked up and smiled at him.

"Come on. We're going to a real place. I'm not taking

you into this dive."

"What?"

"I want to take you to a real restaurant. I can afford it, and you are way too beautiful for this place. You'd clash with the wallpaper.

Austin couldn't suppress her grin. "I was getting ready to tell you I would buy you dinner."

"And then say it's been nice and goodbye?"

"Maybe. Maybe not."

"Let's try maybe not. I promise to be good. Can we please start over?"

"We can try."

"Great, and let's start somewhere memorable."

"What's more memorable than a giant, neon blue dolphin?" she asked.

"Yes, and maybe you can fill me in on that," he said, leading the way to his car.

He drove to a bistro on the lake and had them seated so they had a view of the water, the small dock and the sailboats moored there.

Austin had to agree it provided a nicer atmosphere. After two glasses of wine and an hour of amiable talk she was convinced she had overreacted to Blake's advances.

"Someday I'll be supplying good beef like this to restaurants," he said, stabbing his fork into a piece of fillet mignon.

Austin toyed with her food, nervously rearranging the green beans and swirling butter through the middle of her baked potato.

"You okay?" he asked.

"I don't mean to be such bad company."

"You're not. I'm glad you're here. You just seem miles away."

"Just a lot of things going on lately."

"I know, first your employee, now your brother. It's awful. You must be scared all the time."

"No. I'm fine, really. I think I'm pretty safe. Everyone seems to think it was Will, another of my employees, who's responsible for all of this. Everyone is looking for him, and of course that means they are keeping an eye on my house and the nursery, so I feel pretty safe. Besides, now that we know there's a problem we are more on guard. You know what I mean."

"Yes, you're vigilant. I just hope it doesn't last too long."

"Me too. Now can we talk about something else?"

"Of course. What do you want to talk about?"

"Well, you were asking me about Spruce."
"That's right, I was. How about you try to convince me why I want to live here?"

"I thought you already hired a realtor and were looking at property?"

"I am, but so far I haven't had much luck. Maybe I should go somewhere else. Or maybe you can convince me I should stay."

"Do you mean for me or for Spruce?"

"Well, let's start with Spruce and then see where it ends."

"Ok. Well, I've given this some thought, since you asked me the first time. Let's start with why you wouldn't want to stay here."

"Seems like a bad idea for a sales job, but go ahead."

"I will. Well, to start, there's no nightlife to speak of, unless you count the concerts we hold on Tuesday nights. "

Blake smiled as she rolled her eyes.

"Then there's the weather," she continued. "Which is generally lousy. Half the time you freeze, the rest of the time you burn, there is no spring or fall, just summer and winter, often in the same day. The roads are slippery and the snow plows rip them up. And since there's never enough money to get them fixed the pot holes get bigger and bigger. I guess that's pretty much it. Oh, did I mention mosquitoes the size of house flies? "

"You're doing a lovely job. I'm almost convinced to cut and run, but keep going. Tell me why you stay here. Family obligation?"

"Family? No, not me. I came here about five years ago to spend summer break with a friend from college. I guess I always thought it was a beautiful part of the country, but then I realized it was sort of, well, special."

"How so?"

"You'll think I'm making this up, but I can prove it. It's actually well known that if you look at the valley from the air it forms an almost perfect hand. Most maps don't show it. You have to look at one that shows the elevations, a -- what's it called -- a topographical map. Anyway, it's very odd-looking, like a Babe The Blue Ox story come to life. Or like some powerful old Olympian god reached across the Cascade Mountains and patted his hand hard into the ground and said 'Here, this place.' The rivers are even sort of like the lines in your palm."

"So because Spruce is in this valley that's shaped like a hand it makes you feel safe? Like maybe the town is sitting in the hand of God?"

Austin smiled sheepishly. "I never thought of it quite like that but yes, maybe. Of course, that's just one interesting feature. There are other good things."

"Such as?"

"Mountains, hills, trees, rivers, forests, the whole nature thing. If you love camping and hiking, getting away from people, then you'll love it here. Besides, all that bad stuff I told you about…it can all be positive too."

"How?"

"Take the weather. It's lousy, that's for sure. Too hot or too cold and no rain but, hey, that's great. I hate rain. Half the year I can ski. Half the year I can tan. Plus, you kind of feel closer to your neighbors when you've all sat through a week of no power, because the snow has knocked down trees and power lines, and everybody gets together to share candles and batteries. Sometimes it turns into a big party, all lit up with kerosene lamps and someone usually has a guitar, and it's just a lot of fun."

The waitress interrupted Austin's enthusiastic account of power outages by clearing their plates and bringing them the desert menu. They each chose the chocolate cake and ice cream.

"I've talked long enough," Austin said, after the waitress left. "Tell me about this ranch you're going to buy?"

"You sure you want to hear about all that?"

"Positive."

So Blake told her about the kind of land he was looking for, the breed of cattle and the lineage he wanted them to have. He casually included his hopes of finding a wife and the family he hoped would come along in time.

"It sounds great," said Austin. "So different from my

childhood. We moved so much, and we didn't have any relatives to speak of. Mom and Dad were both only children. I think there's a great aunt somewhere, but that's the sum total of my family."

"It must have been tough, never being able to put down roots," said Blake.

"I don't know. I didn't know anything else, and I did get to experience lots of different places and people. After Dad retired I just kept up the tradition. I'd live somewhere for around a year and then move somewhere else. This is the longest I've ever stayed anywhere. I've been here almost five years. It seems sort of strange, and sometimes I start thinking about what it might be like somewhere else. Then I realize how nice it is to see people I know once in a while. You know, just run into someone on the street or in a store and know their name and where they live and what they do.

"It seems very odd to me that some people have known the same people their whole life. How wonderful it must be to have a great big old family home. To have children going to the same school you once attended. You know, to have traditions. You must think I'm very old-fashioned."

"No. Not at all. Traditions and family are the most important things in the world. Why do you think I'm being so careful about the ranch I buy? It has to be perfect because I intend to live on it and die on it, and I want to pass it on to my children someday."

The waitress brought their desert and Austin found that her appetite had come back. As before, Blake's wishes seemed to reverberate in tandem with her own plans and goals, her own dreams.

She thought about Mark. He was so easy to be with. He made her laugh but, well, he was her therapist, and that was that. Surely his business ethics would not allow him to pursue a relationship with her.

Blake, on the other hand, was not only available, he was as close to the picture she carried in her head of the ideal man as she could imagine. He was masculine, but not insensitive or unable to share his feelings. Most importantly, he seemed sincere about wanting to sink deep roots in the very place that was the first place she'd ever called home. She'd be an idiot to ignore all that, just because of some silly infatuation with Mark.

Chapter 24

After dinner Blake drove Austin back to the parking lot of the Dolphin, where she'd left her truck. It was late. The night's darkness was barely constrained by the cones of lamplight in the parking lot. Blake's presence seemed able to keep the surrounding dark from her thoughts. She only noticed it peripherally as she stood by the truck and let him kiss her goodnight.

It was a quick kiss, just a light pressing of his lips to hers. Austin's face grew hot with shame as she remembered her reaction to him at the house. Obviously she had misread the situation. She was just lucky he hadn't decided she was a total waste of his time.

Blake saved her from making another embarrassing apology by mentioning that he had an early meeting scheduled with his realtor. He waited while she started her truck, then climbed back into his small rental car and drove away.

As Austin headed for home, the prospect of another night alone, of facing the darkness and her empty life, filled her thoughts. She allowed herself a rare moment of bitterness and discontent, dwelling on the unfairness of her phobia and the way it had complicated her life. Tears welled in her eyes. She blinked them away, then forced herself to think of more substantive things, like hiring new employees and ways to make payroll. The distraction helped.

Once home, Austin pulled off her boots and headed for the kitchen to get a glass of water. The phone rang just as she walked past it, the sudden noise making her jump.

"Hello?"

"Austin, hey, it's Will."

"Will?"

"Yes, it's me. Are you surprised? You sound sort of out of breath."

She ignored that and demanded, "Where the hell are you? Why did you take off? Do you know what everyone thinks? What I started to think?"

"I'm sorry, Austin. I'm really sorry. I guess I just got scared."

"So, where are you hiding now? Another empty truck?"

"No, I'm home." Austin was sure she heard a note of glee in his voice as he delivered this bombshell. "I'm at my father's place."
"What!"

"I know. Kind of blows my mind too. After I left I couldn't decide what to do. I thought about turning myself in. I thought about running. Instead I walked down to the highway, thinking I'd hitch a ride out of town. After about five miles I thought I was going to freeze to death, just curl up in a ditch and hope someone found my body in the spring so they could tell my father. Then I got to thinking about him, about how afraid I was of him, and I didn't know why really. After all, he's not sub-human or anything. He doesn't have that much power over me. I mean, I left and got a job and took care of myself for several years. So what if I had to go to jail for a while for stealing his stupid car. At least then it would be over.

"Well, the next car that came by stopped. It was a medical supply salesman going all the way to Sacramento. It was like a sign or something. Once I got to Sacramento I called my dad and he was actually home, on Thanksgiving break. That was like another sign. Anyway, he came and picked me up."

"Will, that's great."

"Yeah. It was pretty cool. Turned out he never called the cops on me either. He said he was ranting about it, and maybe that's where Rosie got the idea, but he didn't do it. So all this time I've been hiding out for nothing. Funny, huh?"

"A real riot," Austin said dryly. "What about the police here in Spruce? You're still running from the scene of a murder, for all they know."

"Nah, my dad's attorneys called them this morning. I have to write something up about what I saw, and I might have to come up there if there are more questions or a trial or something, but for now I'm not even a suspect, especially since I was here when your brother got attacked. They think it's the same person, you know. I mean, they think whoever killed Bunny probably attacked you and your brother too."

"Do they? I think so too, but the police haven't talked to me about their theories. Seems strange that you know more than me, given that I'm right here and you're there."

"Well, being a senator's son does have its perks."

"I suppose. Well, I guess you won't be coming back then. It'll be hard to find someone to replace you."

"Replace me? That'll be impossible."

Austin laughed politely, though she didn't feel the least bit amused. "You take care of yourself," she told him. "Call once in a while, so I know you're doing all right."

"I will," he promised. "And you watch out. Until they find the nut job who's doing this, you could be in danger."

"I'll be careful."

Austin hung up the phone and got her glass of water. As she turned back to the kitchen, a movement beyond the living room window caught her eye. Usually Austin kept the living room curtains, all the curtains, tightly drawn at night. Tonight, however, she had come home late from her dinner with Blake and hadn't thought of it. The living room lights reflected back from the windows, which acted more like mirrors. Austin wondered if what she'd seen hadn't just been her own reflection. That was probably it. No reason to look out there.

Setting the glass of water down hard enough to make some of its contents slosh across her hand, Austin walked quickly across the living room and drew the curtains across the wide picture window. Despite the bright yard light at the end of the driveway, she knew that the darkness was fighting to get in. It stood beneath the trees and was woven within the branches of the shrubs in the yard. Even the grass, each individual stem, cast its own knife-thin blade of darkness.

Once the living room curtains were drawn, Austin moved to close the blinds over the kitchen window and then methodically closed the curtains across every window. As she did, she turned on every light in the house.

Once she was finished, she felt better. She took small sips of water, concentrating on the sensation of swallowing. She had learned this narrowing of focus from one of her counselors. It usually helped, and this time was no exception. Her hands began to steady and her pulse slowed. She took a deep breath that seemed to reach to the bottom of her lungs. Once she felt the last vestiges of panic subside, she made herself walk to the picture window. Taking another deep breath, she took up the edge of the curtain and slowly moved it aside. Nothing happened. She brought her face slowly to the glass, straining to see past her reflection to the yard beyond.

With her face pressed against the window, she was able to see into the yard. Nothing stirred. The yard light gleamed against the edges of the juniper rail fence around the front of the house, and bits of mica in the sidewalk winked like miniature stars. She tried to remember what she had seen: a bright flash of silver, the impression of something moving past? It didn't make sense. She pulled the curtain back in place.

Chapter 25

In the morning Austin decided she was glad that she was going to open the nursery. Having work to occupy her mind would hopefully stop her overactive imagination. She made a quick call to Josh's, to make sure he was still available to work at the nursery and to let him know she was going to pick him up. Josh's father answered, and promised to roust him from his warm bed and make sure he was ready when she arrived.

Finally, she called Muncie. Not to ask for his help, or even to pester him again about how he was doing, but to tell him about Will's phone call. She got his voicemail again. Annoyed, she left a message telling him all that Will had said and warning him to be careful of anyone he saw, since obviously Will was not the person to be wary of.

Eager to get to work and share Will's call with everyone, Austin filled her thermos, grabbed an apple from a fruit bowl on the kitchen table, and hurried out.

Instead of turning left and toward town she turned right and headed around the gentle curve that led around the hill behind her house. Halfway up the hill she turned into the private drive that led to Josh's house. It took her between fields dotted with sheep and into the circular driveway in front of the house. Josh was standing on the wide front porch in a gray plaid jacket and a pulled-down black knit cap. He bounded down the stairs and Austin, glad she didn't have to climb out into the cold, leaned over and unlocked the passenger door. On the way, she told Josh she expected it would be a quiet day. She would take it slowly and teach him something about the usual routines.

Her expectations proved to be wrong. Word had gotten out about the murder of Bunny and the attack on Muncie. But instead of keeping customers away, it seemed to attract them. They wandered through the store and out to the back lot, where yellow tape, still crisscrossed over the potting shed door, fluttered in the breeze. Most of her customers talked openly with Austin, asking questions and offering theories. A popular one was that Will was the murderer. Austin used the opportunity to spread word of his innocence.

At noon Janice came in during a long lunch break. She volunteered to stay and help for as long as she could and she also promised to help more during Christmas break. At present she was a little too busy to be much help. Her class had taken a large role in the holiday productions and there were rehearsals and practices. Austin felt terrible that Janice was apologizing for not being able to take on what was, after all, Austin's responsibility.

Muncie appeared soon after Janice left and asked Austin if she'd had time for lunch yet. Busy ringing up a purchase, she shook her head and said, "There is no way in the world I've got time for lunch unless I order a pizza or something. Of course, you might want to play big brother and run downtown and buy me a burger or three?"

"I suppose I can do that. I got your message, by the way."

"And? What do you think?"

"I don't buy it. I think the little creep did it, and his dad is covering his ass. I'll be back with your lunch in a few."

The grapevine would be twining through town at the speed of sound, thought Austin, looking at the pleased expressions on the faces of the customers who'd overheard. It was a good thing that Will was safely in California and it wasn't the eighteen hundreds, or surely her customers would have had Will tried and hung by nightfall.

Muncie returned just long enough to drop off a bag with burgers and fries. He said he had a lot of work to do at The Lake House. "The electricians are there today," he reassured Austin, seeing the stricken look on her face. "I won't be alone."

Austin nodded her reluctant acceptance. After all, they did have to get on with their lives. Still, she couldn't help but send a silent prayer of safety after him.

At four, her regular work day over, Janice showed up again and jumped right in to help. She was everywhere, helping customers take plants down from overhead, hauling bags of potting soil, sweeping up spills, handing out cups of coffee. Her curly red hair and bright green sweater moved in a blur, as she practically ran to fulfill the customer's needs. What made her especially popular was her willingness to share the experience of being one of the first to see Bunny's body.

At six twenty-five, after the last straggler had been politely asked to leave and the doors were closed and locked, Austin, Janice, and Josh found seats and settled wearily into them.

"Janice, you were fantastic," said Austin. I've never seen anyone work so hard. "If you were a man I'd marry you."

"If I was a man I wouldn't work that hard."

"I think I'll go out back and grab a smoke," said Josh. "It doesn't feel safe in here." He got up, stretched and headed for the back.

"Josh," Austin said anxiously.

"Yeah?"

"Would you mind going out front instead?" She gestured toward the front lot, where he would be plainly in sight through the sliding glass doors.

He hesitated a moment and then nodded. "Sure." Austin sighed as he stepped outside and leaned against the tailgate of her truck in full view.

"That was an incredible day," said Janice, rolling her shoulders and then her head. "I can't believe you do this all the time. I'm all kinks and knots."

Stress lessening, Austin undid the bun at the back of her head and combed her long hair with her fingers.

"Well, it's going to stay like this until I can hire someone. You said you'd think about it. Anyone come to mind?"

"Actually yes, my friend, Shellie. She works at Century 21 Real Estate and is looking for something part time for the winter," offered Janice. "Real estate is real slow right now, and I know she could use the money. She has something like seven kids and her husband's totally worthless. Well, except for making babies, I guess."

"Tell her to call me."

"I will. So, how are you? Are you still seeing Mark?" Janice asked.

"I am. He's great."

"And sexy," added Janice.

"Incredibly sexy," agreed Austin. "You ever notice how he smells, like pine needles and snow or something?"

"Oh boy."

"Hey, I'm supposed to fall for my therapist, right?"

"How should I know? I'm not a nut case."

Austin took a red velvet bow from a stack of them near the box she was sitting on and threw it at Janice. It flew about half the short distance before flopping to the floor.

"Well, that was pathetic," Janice said gleefully.

Austin laughed. "I'm really glad you're my friend."

"Don't go getting weird on me now."

"I'm not. I just wanted you to know. Also, how about loaning me a few dollars. There's this absolutely sweet pair of shoes at Claire's. I've just got to have."

"Did you just use the word 'sweet' to describe a pair of shoes?" asked Janice. "I think I'm going to be sick. Plus, I actually fell for that whole, 'I'm so glad you're my friend' garbage. It was all a setup."

"It was."

"Well, how about falling for one of mine?" asked Janice.

"Depends on what it is."

"Remember me telling you about the Christmas play my class is putting on?"

"Did you just end a sentence with a preposition, school teacher?"

"Let me fix that. Remember me telling you about the Christmas play my class is putting on, bitch?"

"Better. What kind of Christmas play? A baby Jesus kind of thing?"

"No, it's more diverse than that. We're going to have a parade of cultures with kids dressed in costumes representing different beliefs."

"That sounds slightly more interesting."

"The word is progressive. Anyway, the play is next month. They're giving me use of the gym, which sounds good but it's a lot of space to decorate. You want to help?"

"Sure, it sounds like fun," said Austin

"Just remember, you're the one who said fun, not me."

Chapter 26

Three weeks had gone by since Muncie was attacked and life had begun to get back to normal. Austin somehow managed to get through Thanksgiving, with its festive decorations and a message of thanks she certainly wasn't able to feel. She hadn't felt like celebrating at all, but Janice invited her and Muncie to dinner and she had ended up having a nice, if pensive day.

The best thing that had happened lately was her new employee, Shellie, who seemed to be working out well. She was friendly to the customers, unfailingly honest, and despite the expectation that having seven children might affect her punctuality, she had shown up for work reliably every day.

The other bright spot in Austin's world was helping Janice with her Christmas play.

The school had let Janice have use of the gym on Friday, which meant she had only Thursday afternoon and evening to put her decorations in place. Muncie had helped by cutting out the plywood backdrops but they still needed to be carried into the gym and set in place.

Struggling to move the colorfully painted panels into the gym made Austin feel that life was finally beginning to return to normal. After the last cloth was draped around the base of one of the many religious symbols, artfully hiding the raw truth of lumber and nails, Austin stood back to admire her work. The colorful strands of lights they'd laid out along the children's route looked better than she'd expected.

Janice was hanging a strand of small white lights, meant to represent stars, from the ceiling. "Hey," she called down from the top of the scaffolding. "We're about done here. How about I buy you that milk and cookies I promised?"

"You mean you want me to fetch and carry for you?"

"Correct. That would earn you an A plus. Do you mind?"

"Yes, but does it matter?"

"You remember how to get to the kitchen?" Janice called.

"I'll just follow my instincts." Austin shouted back, her voice echoing from the walls. She didn't like that. Didn't like the hollow sound her shoes made as she walked down the long hallway toward the kitchen either. But there was plenty of light. Hard and white, it bounced off the worn yellow and black speckled floor tiles and illuminated the rows of predominately green and red construction paper art. The season was obvious. Austin admired the pictures of Santa and Mrs. Claus, elves, and snowmen and Christmas trees paper clipped to strings of yarn stretched along the walls.

Clever, she thought, no tape on the walls, no tacks to tick off the janitor. She almost missed the door to the kitchen and had to backtrack. It was a long narrow room with two double sinks, a commercial-sized dishwasher, walls of metal cupboards and drawers, and a long center island. Everything one would need to feed two hundred and fifty elementary school kids lined the walls and filled the cabinets.

A little overwhelmed by the sheer amount of stuff, Austin decided they would be uncivilized and eat their cookies out of the bags they brought them in. She would just need to find glasses for their milk. On her fourth cabinet she found the glasses and set them on the island. The milk would be in the refrigerator of course, but when Austin opened what she thought was the refrigerator it turned out to be a huge freezer, stocked to bursting with packages wrapped in white paper.

"Strange. I wonder where. . ." There was a door beside the freezer. Maybe it led to another room where they kept the refrigerators. She pulled it open and a wave of cold air swept over her.

"Wow!" She stepped inside a room that looked like a pantry but felt like a refrigerator. The walls were lined with deep shelves painted gloss white and lined with newspaper. They held bins of vegetables, fruits, bottles upon bottles of juice, and several gallon jugs of milk.

"There you are." Austin realized she was talking out loud to herself. She decided the school was so eerily quiet that she was doing it just to fill the silence. She chose a bottle of milk that had already been opened, unscrewed the lid and sniffed to see if it was fresh, then took a last look around the refrigerator. She wondered if they were all like this or if this was just such an old school that—

The door slammed shut behind her. The sudden change in pressure actually made her ears hurt for a moment. She nearly dropped the milk. Then she set it down carefully and took a deliberate step to the door. "It's just a spring loaded door, that's all. They probably built it like that so people wouldn't leave it open and spoil the food." She had so thoroughly convinced herself that when it refused to open, she was actually surprised.

"This isn't fair," she said to no one in particular, her voice rising with each word. "Do you hear me? This isn't fair. Let me out. Let me out right now." She rattled the cold metal doorknob. It jiggled up and down and turned freely, but the door would not open. She turned away to look for something to pound on the door. Janice would hear her. Of course she would. She would be here any moment. Austin fought back the building panic. One of the vegetable bins should make a hell of a lot of noise. She dumped one out. Potatoes bounced and rolled across the floor. She turned back toward the door and the lights went out.

"I knew you would," she shrieked. "I just knew you would." She drew back the vegetable bin, plastic, and not as heavy as she would have liked, and smashed it into the door. It didn't make much noise but it did seem to drain all of her energy. She slid to the floor, her back against the door, her hands flat on the floor at each side of her as she fought for balance against the waves of dizziness that finally overcame her, taking her to that place where there was no fear.

Chapter 27

It barely surprised Austin to come to and find herself lying on top of the center island in the big, empty kitchen. In a way, she had come to expect this sort of thing. Her acceptance of the strange occurrences in her life, her unique relationship with time and memory, bothered her. It was as if she had given up in some way— had accepted a measure of helplessness.

When she woke her first awareness had been of the stainless steel island, cold and hard beneath her. She opened her eyes and blinked against the harsh lights. Then she rolled over and sat up, her legs dangling, and slipped off the table and onto her feet. She felt a little woozy, and reached for the island to steady her balance. This was the way she always felt after one of her "episodes." She knew the feeling would pass. She would just have to endure if for a short time, the way she imagined diabetics endured jabbing a needle into their own bodies, a momentary discomfort to be forgotten until the next time. But at least they had control, she thought enviously.

How long had this one lasted, she wondered, and what

damage had she done to get free? Her thoughts still hazy, she started to walk toward the refrigerated room to check, but her shoe caught on something. She looked down and saw a strip of duct tape dangling from the toe of her shoe. She reached down and pulled it off, balled it up, and absently shoved it into the pocket of her jeans.

The refrigerator seemed fine. The floor was still littered with potatoes, and the vegetable bin she'd used to hit the door had a crack down one side. The part of her that hated chaos wanted to go in and pick up the potatoes and set things right, but she knew there was no way she could bring herself to step inside that room again. That room! She had been trapped. There had been darkness. Where was he? Where was the man who locked her inside and turned off the lights? At least Muncie was safe. He had not come to the school with her. It had only been her and Janice. Janice! Austin tried to run, but her legs were half numb. She lurched from the kitchen into the hall.

"Janice!" she yelled, her voice bouncing from the walls and echoing down the long hallway.

Stumbling down the hallway, weaving erratically, Austin reached for the wall to restore her balance. A child's rendering of reindeer tore free and fluttered to the floor, but she didn't notice.

As she pushed through the double doors and into the gym, she noticed the overhead lights had been turned off but the room sparkled with Christmas lights, a dazzling display of color. Austin looked up to where she had last seen Janice at the top of the scaffold. There was a tangled cluster of white lights there and a wide swath of darkness. It looked as if a whole section had come down. Austin moved closer, and finally saw Janice.

She knew it was Janice. You recognize your best

friend, even if her face is gone.

Austin screamed, she screamed and then she turned to run and ran right into his chest. He grabbed her by the arms with a grip so tight she knew there was no hope. She knew it was her turn, that whatever he had done to Janice he would now do to her, but she would not fight. In fact, she would welcome the end. Let it be over. Let it finally be finished. She closed her eyes, sinking into that dark place she knew so well hoping this time, she would not return.

After a long time she realized she was sitting in a chair with her head down between her knees, and someone was waving smelling salts under her nose.

Eventually it occurred to her that the smelling salts were gone and she was sitting up in a chair with her hands over her face, gently rocking back and forth. "Her face. Her face. Where is her face?" she had been chanting it until the words lost their meaning and became nonsense syllables, a mantra of protection. Her voice was hoarse, a harsh whisper she barely recognized. Her throat hurt from the strain of her screams. She would have laryngitis for a week.

At some point, Mark arrived. He took her hands. She opened her eyes and he was kneeling at her feet. "Listen," he said. "Her face is not gone. He wrapped duct tape around her head. You hear me? Her face is there. It was just the tape you saw."

"She's okay?"

"No, Austin. She's dead. You have to come out of it and deal with that."

"Duct tape?" There was something about duct tape but it eluded her. The harder she tried to think about it, the more slippery it seemed to get.

"A friend of mine, Doctor Shapiro, gave you an

injection. You might be feeling a little strange right now. Just let yourself go. Let yourself relax. I'm sending you to the hospital. You've had a bad shock."

"He was here. He grabbed me."

"No Austin. He didn't grab you. You must have found Janice and screamed. The janitor heard you. Then you ran into the hallway and right into him. He didn't try to grab you. It was just the janitor. He was as scared as you were."

"I want to go home," Austin said.

"You will. Tomorrow."

She remembered being alone then for a while, or maybe it had been before. She remembered uniformed officers walking past. She recalled shiny black shoes, the smell of cigarettes, bits of conversation. "Hung up just like a freaking piñata. Whacked her in the head over and over just like—" but then someone had shushed him. She remembered other things as well: twinkling lights, white sheets, the smell of disinfectant and then the welcome slide into a drug-induced sleep as deep as a coma.

When she woke up they gave her a cup of coffee and she burned her lip. The pain was the first sensation that had seemed real since she had seen Janice's body, wrapped in blinking white lights, swinging slowly beside the scaffolding.

Later that morning a police detective interviewed her. Lying in the narrow hospital bed, in an unfamiliar room and with the remnants of the tranquilizer making it hard to focus, Austin felt disoriented and vulnerable.

She noticed the detective had big hands and a bloody red spot in his eye like you can get from coughing or throwing up too hard. He smelled like stale cigarettes, wool, and aftershave that was too sweet. She found that, by concentrating on each little detail, her thoughts became more clear. She answered his questions in a forced whisper.

When he finally ran out of questions and left, she climbed out of bed and found the locker where her clothes had been neatly folded and stacked. She reached into the pocket where she'd put it and found the flattened ball of duct tape. She carried it to the bathroom, closed the door behind her and leaned against it. She held the ball of tape up to the light, turned it this way and that. It was almost as if she were willing it to speak to her. If that was what she expected, then she was disappointed. It told her nothing. She tossed it in the garbage.

An hour later the same detective returned with another man and a woman. He introduced them as the forensic team from Medford. They took Austin's clothes and placed them in plastic bags, took scrapings from under her nails and told her they had arranged for blood samples to be drawn and sent to their lab. They asked if she had any questions. She did not.

After they left she returned to the bathroom and fished the ball of duct tape out of the garbage. After hesitating for just a moment, she dropped it into the toilet and flushed, watching to make sure it was gone.

Mark arrived while Austin was forcing herself to eat a hospital lunch of limp macaroni and cheese and juice that tasted like the plastic cup it was served in. He had a bag of her clothes with him.

"I got in touch with your brother," he explained, "and he put a few things together for you. How are you feeling?"

"Better," Austin answered. "Still a little shaky, but better. Have the police talked to you?"

"Not today."

"Do they think I had something to do with Janice?"

"I don't think so," Mark said reassuringly.

"Is the janitor all right?"

"I believe he is. Though you did scare the hell out of him."

"I'm sorry."

"It's OK. I'm sure he'll make a full recovery. It's you we're worried about right now. You've had a pretty rough time."

Austin shuddered as the memory of Janice, hanging from the ceiling, her features obscured by several wraps of duct tape, so that it appeared as if someone had removed her face. She rubbed her arms briskly, trying to erase the cold, and the vision.

"When I ran into him I guess it was natural for him to put his arms out. I thought he was trying to hold me. I thought he was the killer. I need to go home." Austin declared. "Can I go home, or are you holding me for the police?"

"Not at all," Mark said, putting his hand on hers and giving it a reassuring squeeze, "You're here voluntarily and can leave whenever you want. Are you sure you're feeling strong enough to go home?"

"Yes." Austin asserted. "I need to be around my own things, in my own house. Besides, I have a business to run. It won't run itself, and this is a very busy season for us. Work will…well, it will keep my mind off other things. Do you understand?"

"Of course I do." He patted her arm. "You seem to know what you need, so let's not try to second guess you. I'll go hunt up a nurse and we'll do what we have to to get you out of here. Okay?"

Chapter 28

Austin hadn't been able to think clearly that night in the hospital, but that morning, as she waited to be discharged, she found herself with nothing else to do but think. What she wanted was to find a pattern. There must be a pattern and a reason for the things that were happening to the people around her.

She considered Will first. Muncie seemed so sure of Will's guilt. Could he be right? Had she been allowing her emotions to rule her and believe Will too quickly?

If she assumed that all four of the events were tied together and that the same person was responsible, then she had to rule Will out. The police had assured her that he had been in California when Janice was killed.

Austin was discharged at two o'clock and Mark drove her home. She said goodbye to him quickly, almost rudely, but with many reassurances. Then she made a quick call to Muncie to let him know she was fine and to thank him. He had thoughtfully had her pickup driven home. As soon as she had finished with those obligations she fixed a thermos of coffee, grabbed a half-full bag of chocolate chip cookies from the cupboard, and climbed in her truck. She munched on the cookies and sipped the coffee as she drove to Moon Meadow.

Snow had turned the unplowed parking area into a glistening white table crisscrossed with tire tracks. Her tires crunched across the thin layer of ice that crusted the inches of powder underneath. There was plenty of traction, but she still drove in slowly and pumped her brakes as she pulled up and parked near the dock. Hers was the only car in sight. She was alone, the quiet nearly absolute, except for the ticking of her truck's cooling engine and somewhere, beyond the tree line, a snapping, clattering sound. Probably a small herd of deer disturbed by her presence and moving deeper into the woods, or maybe just a tree bending and breaking under the weight of the snow, she decided.

Getting out of the truck, Austin noticed that the wind was picking up. Its icy touch made her skin sting and her lips feel raw. She took a few deep breaths, taking the chill air deep into her lungs. It felt as if she was letting out the antiseptic stink of the hospital, but she could only stand it a moment before climbing back into the warmth of the truck's cab.

Sitting quietly she watched as the slanting rays of the sun glinted across the river, the sky slowly turning from powder blue to emerald blue with streamers of pink, but she wasn't really seeing the spectacular sunset. Instead, she was busily considering a pattern.

When Bunny was killed that Saturday night, where had she been? She had been lying on the floor of her bedroom, unconscious and in the dark. For how long?

When Muncie was attacked, she had been unconscious. Evidence showed she had escaped the basement. Was that after Muncie was attacked, or before?

When Janice was killed, she had been unconscious again, trapped in the refrigerated room. She had awoken in the kitchen, with no memory of how she got there, but with a strip of duct tape attached to her shoe.

Had she used the tape to hide her best friend's features so she could kill her more easily?

She had sort of joked with Mark, at one of their sessions, about the possibility of an evil spirit, an entity born in the darkness of the bomb shelter. She had thought of it as separate, a distinct organism that acted on its own. What if the thing did exist, but not alone? What if it needed her to act because it was hiding inside her?

Everything had begun to happen after she was locked in the potting shed. Did it wake up then?

Had there been something in that bomb shelter after all, something that stayed in the background waiting and hoping to be freed.? What if her panic attacks, the fear that drove her mind to escape to a place deeper than sleep was what it needed to awake? Did it take over the use of her body and filled with evil intent did it then attack and kill those around her?

No. That was crazy. Was she really losing her mind? Things like that don't exist. She tried shaking off the thought, though once given form it wouldn't fade so easily. Starting the truck, she drove toward home. The unwanted thoughts traveled with her, as constant and unrelenting as anything she might have met once, in the dark.

Chapter 29

In the morning the phone woke Austin. Answering, she found Josh's father on the other end.

"How can I help you, Mr. Mikkelson?" she asked.

"Have you seen Josh?" he asked, concern roughening his voice.

Austin was suddenly wide awake. "No, I haven't. I haven't seen him since…since Thursday morning, the day. . ."

"Yes, we heard about your friend. I'm very sorry to hear about it, and now I'm getting a little scared. I had some concern about Josh working for you after what happened to his coworker, and then your friend, and now it looks like he's disappeared."

"When?" she asked.

"He left Thursday night on his bike. Said he was going for a ride, but I imagine he was heading to town to get another pack of cancer sticks. Wife and I went to bed, and when we got up, there was no sign of him. Didn't worry us at first. Figured he went in to work early. Then we heard on

194

the news about your friend getting killed. Called the nursery and found out it was closed. That's when we started to get—well, we're worried," he admitted.

"The police?" Austin asked, climbing out of bed and sliding her feet into her slippers.

"They told us at first they couldn't count him missing for several more hours. Then we told them he worked for you and they got busy and started looking. Haven't heard nothing. I left a message on your phone."

"I haven't been checking it."

"I figured."

"What can I do?" Austin asked.

"Just let me know if you see him, that's all."

"I promise, Mr. Mikkelson," she said. "I'm so sorry."

"Nothing to be sorry for."

There was a click as he hung up the phone. Numbed by this last blow, Austin found it difficult at first to get through her morning routine. Part of her wanted to go back to bed, to sink into the blissful peace of sleep, to forget about Josh missing and Janice and Bunny gone forever. By the time she was dressed and had coffee she had given up on sleep. She was sick and tired of sitting around waiting to see what would happen next. She started by calling the police, working through the levels of bureaucracy until she reached Detective Clark.

"This is Austin Ward," she said, though she was sure he'd been told who was calling. "Two people I care the most about in this world are dead. My brother was almost killed, and now someone who works for me is missing. What are you doing about it?"

"I assure you that we are investigating."

"Investigating who? I mean, who is left to investigate?" She slammed the phone down, knowing what she had just done was stupid and childish, nothing more than a temper tantrum, directed toward the person who was probably working hardest. No doubt she'd apologize for her outburst at some point in the future, but for the moment she felt a little better. Now, to do something a little less pointless.

Digging out her photo albums, she looked for pictures taken at one of the summer barbecues. She sifted through them until she found a clear shot of Josh.

Thinking how shocking her plan could be to the Mikkelsons, she called them.

"Marga?"

"Yes?" The voice was hesitant, quavering and sounded very frail. Austin knew Marga as a strong woman, as tall as her husband and as hard a worker. She drove a school bus and kept the kids in line with one look. She kept a meticulous home, a garden that provided vegetables to all the neighbors, including Austin, and helped out with the sheep whenever needed.

"It's Austin." She hesitated. Then: "I've had no news. I only called to see. . .to tell you, rather, that I am making flyers, you know, to hang around town. I'm going to ask that anyone who saw him to call me."

"Do you believe this will help?"

"Yes. At least I think so," Austin said, afraid to offer even this slender hope, but unable not to.

"I pray you are right. We are not so good here."

"I know. I'm sorry. I'll let you know as soon as I hear from anyone."

"Thank you. We will be waiting."

Austin drove to The Copy Shoppe on Main Street.

They had printed flyers and business cards for her before and she knew they did good work. She asked for fifty copies and taped the first one in the window of the shop. Then, armed with a roll of masking tape, Austin began to walk, stopping at the end of every block to either hang a sign in a conveniently located store or, if there was none, to tape one to a telephone pole or whatever surface was available.

She was illegally taping a flyer to the side of a blue mail receptacle outside the barber shop when she felt a presence. Turning, she saw Mark standing and watching her.

"I think the post office folks frown on that," he said.

"So?"

"Can I help?" he asked.

Pushing her damp bangs off her forehead, Austin nodded gratefully and said, "I thought this was a small town. I'm not halfway done and I'm wearing out."

"We'll use my car. I'll drive, you tape," Mark offered.

"That would be great. First stop, we need to go get some more copies made."

"Stay here. I'll pick you up." Mark turned and walked down a side street. In a moment he was back, pulling alongside and opening the Jeep's passenger side door.

"You look hot," Mark said, as she slid inside and shut the door. "I mean flushed," he quickly corrected himself.

"I knew what you meant," she said, giving him a small smile. "My face is hot, and I'm sweating, but my feet are wet and freezing. This little heat wave is creating a messy thaw. I'm getting sunburned and standing in slushy snow and melting ice at the same time."

"Sounds like fun."

"Well, at least it feels like I'm doing something, instead of just sitting around waiting for the next disaster," Austin said. "My therapist would no doubt approve."

"I'm sure," answered Mark, "and so does your friend."

Having made this statement, Mark slid the Jeep into first gear.

Chapter 30

Austin opened the nursery early the following Tuesday, just one day after Janice's funeral and five days since she had found her body.

Some thought it was too early. Others realized it was the best thing she could do to keep from dwelling on the terrible things that had happened in her life. How she was handling this last tragedy, the disappearance of another employee, was the subject of much conjecture and concern.

Her regulars, the customers who knew her, came in throughout the day, pushing their cars and trucks through four inches of new powder. They bought poinsettias and twine, gloves and bulbs. They all knew what had happened to Janice. The details of her death had made the news, yet no one asked about it. No one, seeing Austin's pale face, and her red-rimmed eyes, could mistake the fact of her mourning.

Josh's disappearance was another matter entirely. Several customers asked if they'd received any calls yet. Austin realized that they had seen the posters she and Mark had put up all over town, in some way that had made it a public matter that they felt free to speak to her about.

Austin avoided ringing up customers as best she could, concentrating on putting together garlands from boughs provided by their Christmas tree man, Ben, who had set up on the far side of the parking lot and seemed to be doing a brisk business now that it was only three days to Christmas.

After the garlands were tied together, Austin added red bows and shiny ornaments. Then with Shellie's help they sprayed the garlands with artificial snow. They were selling as fast as she could put them together. and Shellie had just left with an armful of garlands to deliver to the tree stand when Paco walked in.

"Paco! she exclaimed, "How nice to see you."

"You too," Paco said. "Can we speak?"

"We can try. It's quiet for the moment, but you know how it goes."

"Yes, I do. May I?" he asked, gesturing toward the coffee maker.

"Sure," Austin said.

Paco poured himself a cup of coffee, added creamer and three packets of sugar. Austin could see he was killing time, gathering his thoughts and his words. She waited patiently, her fingers busy tying wire to pinecones.

"This is a very hard thing to say. We have worked well together, I think," Paco finally said.

Austin nodded. Afraid that she could guess where this was leading.

Paco sipped his coffee, then set it on the counter.

"My wife's sister has asked me to come to work for her husband at his store. He has been sick with his heart and needs help. Also, the store is a good business. It will pay more than I make now. Also, we will live in an apartment above my wife's sister and it is bigger than our house here."

"Also people are not being beaten to death, one after another, or disappearing, never to be seen again. Sounds like a step up to me," Austin added. It was meant to be a light statement, a show of understanding, but bitterness turned her smile into something ugly.

She turned away from him, hot tears springing to her eyes. Knuckling them away, embarrassed and surprised by her intense reaction, she said, "Well, I never thought you'd stay forever. Then she turned back around to face him. This time, her smile was genuine. "I'll miss you, though."

"And I will miss you."

There was no talk of writing letters or exchanging emails.

Paco put his hand out to shake hers and she ignored it, stepping forward to hug him hard instead. He hugged her back, a quick affectionate squeeze.

The tears returned as Austin watched him walk across the parking lot and climb into his truck for the last time. She brushed them away again. There would be no falling apart. She had done that once, and where had she landed but the hospital? She didn't want to go back there and even more, she didn't want to feel like she was no longer in control of her life.

Still, she knew she had a lot to deal with. Every thought, every memory of Janice brought sadness and a kind of pain that washed through her, real physical pain.

She would have to keep seeing Mark—as much as she hated admitting that she was not okay and that she couldn't do this alone. On top of that she had all but made up her mind to quit seeing him professionally and then, after a reasonable amount of time, if she continued to think about him, to call him, ask him out. That idea was out.

Of course, there was also Blake. Though she wasn't sure if her attraction to him was anything more than physical, she wanted to find out. He had been so attentive, so concerned, especially after Janice . . . He had done everything right, but Mark still connected with her on some deeper level, some wordless place that she went to when she met his gaze. She thought he must feel it too, that sense of connection. But of course his ethics would never allow him to admit to anything more than a professional relationship or a casual friendship. Worst of all, she knew how weak she was now. How fragile her mind, how strong her need. Was she healthy enough to be involved in any kind of relationship?

In spite of her feelings, or perhaps because of them, Mondays had become her lifeline. Monday was the day she saw Mark.

Chapter 31

On Monday afternoon she climbed the stairs to Mark's office and, as usual, her depression seemed to lift a little. She was feeling brave today. Brave enough to be honest and reveal how badly messed up she was. At least she liked to believe she was that brave.

Beginning slowly, she started by talking about the bomb shelter again, and the accident that had caused her to develop a fear of the dark and of closed spaces.

"How did you deal with it when you were young?" Mark asked.

"It got in the way lots of times," she admitted. I could go out and play at night, as long as there were street lights or porch lights, but you know kids. They like to do scary things. Hide in the dark. I couldn't do those things. I couldn't play hide and seek or have sleepovers in the back yard, nothing like that."

"You got scared," he said.

"If the conditions were right. But it was more than just feeling afraid. I had panic attacks. Full-blown attacks, complete with hyperventilating, blackouts, memory loss.

The other kids would figure out pretty fast that I was weird, but then we'd move and there would be a whole new set of kids and sort of a grace period before they started to figure it out."

"You seem to have adjusted very well."

"I guess you can learn to adapt to anything. I learned how to avoid situations where I would feel panicked. I stay out of elevators. I keep flashlights in my truck and in several places in my house." For a moment the memory of finding the flashlight in the bedroom, dead and worthless the night of the power outage, flashed through her mind, but she drug herself back to the present and shook it off. "It's so easy to sit here and analyze myself, to sound so rational and composed. The truth is, I'm not sure I'm rational at all. In fact, lately I've been wondering just how sane I am."

Mark sat silent, waiting for her, sensing she had not finished.

She rubbed her hands together, looking down at the carpeting. "It's just the same old thing, monsters in the closet."

She had been so close to telling him what she had begun to suspect: that maybe there really had been something in the dark in the bomb shelter. Was it possible that when she had been locked in, on that terrible winter afternoon, that something had found her? Maybe because she had been so young, or maybe because she had been so terrified, it had found a way in, a weakness that allowed it to enter, to slip in and take over her brain, her soul? And the final fear, the possible truth that had begun to haunt her, was that she was the one who was responsible for all that had been happening. That it was her hand that had stabbed with the trowel, lifted the hammer, wrapped the tape. It was possible. She had no alibi for the times when the attacks occurred. No memory but of darkness. What was she capable of in the dark? She shuddered. Or maybe the thing she had met in the dark had not used her body but passed through her, using her as a gateway. Maybe it was a demon, trapped in hell but through her able to migrate to this plane of existence. These thoughts were so crazy. Did she dare share them?

Mark continued to sit quietly, waiting.

"It's nothing," she finally said. "It's just been a very bad year. So many people have died, yet I find myself crying hardest because my foreman quit."

Chapter 32

Austin drove home slowly, the sound of Mark's reassurances echoing, a hollow sound in her ears. Why hadn't she told him all of her fears? Wasn't that his very purpose? She was disgusted with herself.

The streets were packed with snow and more was falling. Dark clouds were rolling in from the north, carrying the promise of more storms throughout the night. Austin reached into the glove compartment and snapped on the flashlight she kept there. It came on immediately. Satisfied, she put it back. She might not have control, but at least she could stop making more stupid mistakes. She would stay out of closed places and make sure she always had some source of light at hand. She might never overcome her fear of the dark, but at least she could do everything in her power to fight the darkness.

Suddenly, the rear of the pickup slid sideways. She steered into the slide and the vehicle fishtailed, sliding back and forth until finally bouncing off the ridge of snow the plows had left, and coming to a stop in the center of the street. Hands gripping the steering wheel, Austin took a moment to compose herself, then slowly released the brake and touched the gas. The truck moved forward and she drove home carefully.

When she pulled into her driveway she breathed a sigh of relief. Unlocking her front door, she reached in, switched on the lights and then entered. Once more she felt a twinge of regret that she was entering an empty house. She had considered getting a dog, but thought that with her schedule, a dog wouldn't get the attention it needed. "Fish." she said to the stillness. "Maybe I'll just get some fish. They don't bark or shed. Well, I don't think they shed. Boy, you better quit talking to yourself. People will think you are batty." She said this as she hung up her coat, then walked through the living room and into the kitchen. The red light was blinking on her answering machine, so she punched the play button as she went by. She was reaching for a beer and a carton of cold fried chicken when Blake's voice filled the room.

"Hello, sweetheart. How you doing? You doing all right?"

He was drunk. Somewhat amused, Austin put the chicken on the counter and twisted the cap off of the beer.

"You call me, sweetheart. You call me soon's you get in, hear?"

She heard the fumbled clanking as he tried to hang the phone up, and then the tone that said he'd been successful.

"Well, that was weird," she said to no one.

At 1:16 a.m. the phone began to ring. Austin came up out of a deep sleep slowly. Before she was able to fumble for the phone the answering machine pick up. She heard her own voice on the recorded message and then Blake's.

"You didn't call me sweetheart. What you doing? You

207

gonna call? Better call me. You hear me? You there?" There were some mumbled words and then the same disconnect technique.

Austin brushed hair out of her face, groaned and rolled over. Amusement had become annoyance, but only mild annoyance. Within moments she was sleeping.

Austin arrived late for work the next morning. She rarely set an alarm since, an early riser, she didn't usually need one.

"It must have been the middle of the night phone call," she told Shellie. A friend called me in the early, and I mean very early, hours," she explained. I think he was drinking pretty hard. You know how people get when they drink too much. He wanted to talk. Maybe he found a ranch and was celebrating."

"A ranch?"

"Oh yeah, I forget. In your real life you're a realtor. Maybe you've met my friend. His name is Blake. He's been here for six weeks or so, looking for a ranch in the area." "In the area of Blue Spruce?"

"Uh huh."

"Funny, you'd think I'd have heard about him. We specialize in ranch and farm properties, and nothing has sold for a while. In fact, I don't think we've had a call in two months. It gets that way sometimes. Then all hell breaks loose and you close eight properties in a week."

"Well, he must be using a different agency," suggested Austin.

"There's only one other, and we get together for lunch and whatnot. I haven't heard a word about a potential buyer. Well, maybe someone is trying to keep him to themselves. It can be pretty cut-throat," Shellie admitted.

"Oh, by the way, I forgot to tell you. A woman named Granny called. She said you'd know who she was and for you to call her."

"Thanks."

Chapter 33

Austin called Granny, worried that another tragedy loomed. She was more than relieved when Granny asked if she would mind terribly picking up a bottle of gin, since she had run out. "My arthritis is kicking up with all this cold weather. 'Sides, I haven't seen you in what seems like a long time. You just get on over here tonight, there'll be a fine roast in the oven for dinner."

Austin had a quiet dinner with Granny. They talked about the old days, herbs for healing, the changes in the world. Only when it was time to go did Granny mention the string of tragedies and express her sadness at the deaths of Bunny and Janice. Granny hugged her tight, and Austin felt just a tiny bit better, but it was better than she'd felt for a while. It made her grateful and gave her hope that there would be better days.

Austin pulled into her driveway and was surprised to see Blake's rental car parked there. She hadn't spoken to him, and the last she'd heard from him was when he'd last called. Maybe that was why he was here. Maybe he wanted to apologize for the drunken phone calls. That made sense.

She parked beside his car. He wasn't in it. Getting out of the truck she spotted him standing on the front porch, waiting.

"You must be freezing," she said, jangling her keys to show him they'd soon be inside.

"What the hell would you care?" he demanded. "You just pretending to care anyway. You a good little actress, huh?" He brought a bottle of amber liquid to his lips and she saw his throat work as he drank.

"I think you should leave. You're drunk again. Or still. Whichever it is, I don't care."

"No kiddin'. Well, maybe I like drinkin'. Ever thinka' that?"

"Oh, I think I've figured that out. Please go."

"Make me."

"You're being ridiculous. Grow up." She tried to move past him, but he staggered into her path. "Move out of my way, or I'll call the police."

"Don't think so."

"What do you mean? Let go." Blake had lurched forward and grabbed her wrist.

"Don't have a cell phone." His breath was rank with the smell of whiskey.

Austin struggled to pull away but he tightened his grip, grinding the bones of her wrist. She gasped at the sudden pain. He pushed her back against the front door. For the first time she wished her house wasn't so isolated.

"I been real good. I been a real gentleman."

"That's true," she agreed, trying to mollify him. "You have. Why stop now?"

"Cause you damn women don't want gentlemen. No

ma'am, what you want is this." He pushed against her and she twisted aside. He ground his groin against her hip.

Disgusted, Austin tried to pry his fingers from her wrist. He laughed. She changed tactics, pushing instead of pulling, and he gave ground, staggering back one, then two steps, but his grip on her wrist didn't loosen.

Frustrated and growing angry, she slapped at him awkwardly with her left hand. He laughed at her and caught her hand, twisting her fingers until she let out a shriek of pain. He pushed against her again, ramming her back against the door. Her lower back slammed painfully into the doorknob. She whimpered, but tried to knee him in the groin. He turned aside, and she connected with his thigh instead. They were wrestling more than hitting, pulling against each other, pushing. The smell of his damp wool coat was in her nose, mixed with cologne and alcohol. If she could just jerk free, get loose for one minute. He was so drunk she felt sure she could outrun him easily. He seemed to guess her thoughts, and his hand tightened around her wrist.

He was enjoying this, she realized, as she looked up and into his shining eyes, saw his wide grin. He was just playing with her, a nasty game of cat and mouse, and she was the mouse. Well, mice could fight. She bit his face. She felt her teeth sink into the flesh of his jaw, felt her teeth skid against the hardness of bone.

He shrieked and let go. She ducked past him and he reached for her and almost missed, but then his hand caught the ends of her hair. Suddenly she was pulled backward. He got a better grip of her hair and slammed her hard into the front wall of the house. Still using her hair, he drug her to her feet with his left hand, then swung with his right fist and connected with her stomach

She fell to her knees. She couldn't breathe, couldn't catch her breath. He grabbed the collar of her coat and drug her along the porch and into the driveway. She made a ragged, choking sound as she fought to take a breath, just one breath to fill her burning lungs. Suddenly she had it. Greedily she sucked air deep into her lungs and felt strength flowing back into her body, clarity to her mind.

She had to fight. This was not a game she could win unless she fought. Pretending surrender would gain her nothing. Reaching up, she tore at the hand holding her coat, dug her nails into his flesh and kicked at his legs at the same time. He growled a curse she couldn't understand for the blood pounding in her ears and shoved her against the side of his car.

She twisted aside so that she had her back to the car and he was in front of her. He still had the collar of her coat and it was twisted up around her neck, one arm almost free. She decided her best chance was to slide out of the coat entirely.

But he was one thought ahead of her, and when she started to fall he used his hip to slam her into the car and pin her there. Then he took hold of her hair again and turned her and slammed her face first into the trunk of the car. She managed to get an arm up to absorb some of the impact and cushion the force. Even so, she heard a crunching sound, and a bright corona of light dazzled her eyes while pain, as jagged and broken as the bones in her nose, shocked her into stunned helplessness.

She slid to the ground, and he stood on her ankle, keeping her pinned just in case, while he unlocked the trunk of his car. Once he had it open he reached down and almost gently lifted her to her feet. Her knee cracked hard against the bumper as he awkwardly pushed her forward into the trunk.

The fresh pain helped clear her head and she could hear him. Hear his curses. "Billy sitch. All the same. Never fucking learn. Never."

She was inside the trunk now, only her lower legs outside the car. He grabbed her ankles and lifted them into the trunk. She reached up to touch her face, to cup her broken nose. Sticky wet blood ran down her face, the copper taste filled her mouth, made her want to be sick.

Then she realized what he'd said. Eyes wide and pain nearly forgotten she said, "You. You're the boy from Germany, my brother's friend. How?"

"Ah. The secret is out. Yes, that's right. I am the boy. I knew you'd remember me eventually. How very nice to see you again." Blood, seeping from the jagged tear in his face where she had bitten him, sprinkled her as he talked.

Desperately, Austin tried to roll out of the trunk. Blake easily pushed her back in.

"Settle down. You just settle down and stop fighting me or you're gonna get hurt."

"Why? Tell me why you're doing this?" she asked, unbidden tears nearly blinding her.

"I told you. You're all alike. All of you. Stupid billy sitches. Afraid of the dark. Afraid of everything. Stupid worthless cunt." His words, like blows, hammered her. He leaned forward into the trunk just inches from her face and bellowed, "This has all been your fault. Before you, I had a life. Before you, my stupid mother obeyed my father like she was supposed to. Do you understand now? Can you hear me?"

Like some demented drill instructor, with saliva and blood spraying from his mouth, he kept screaming at her, words that meant nothing, nonsense syllables. Then, as suddenly as the tirade began, it stopped, and he grew quiet again.

In a soft whisper, he said, "I have really enjoyed fucking with you. I loved it when I pushed you down the basement stairs. Too bad you didn't break your silly neck. I loved it when I turned off the lights and you screamed for me. Will you scream for me again? I have so enjoyed fucking with you. Do you think I'll enjoy fucking you? Do you? That's what I'm going to do to you, lucky girl. As soon as you are quiet and good, I am going to have a really nice time with you. Then I am going to bury you in a tiny little box deep in the ground but if you're a very nice little girl I might not. I might not put you in that box. You'd like that, wouldn't you? You'd do just about anything to avoid being underground, in the dark. Now am I right?" He licked his lips.

"I don't understand. I don't know why you're doing this."

"All part of the mystery, sweetheart. All part of the freaking mystery. Now, let's go for a little ride, shall we? Not a long ride, but I can guarantee, a dark and rather unpleasant one," and before Austin could react he had reached up and slammed down the trunk lid.

It was dark, too dark. The fear would grow, and she would become helpless. Blake was going to hurt her, rape her, probably kill her if she didn't do something. She had to stay conscious so she could fight him. Be calm, she told herself. Try to think. Light. Flashlight. Matches. Of course, matches. There was a pack of matches in her pocket. She had started carrying them after the night the lights went out and her flashlight had been broken. Hands shaking, she pulled them out of her pocket.

The car started and lurched forward. She was thrown around and hit the side of her head on the underside of the trunk. Pain seared a path behind her eyes; her brain felt like it was on fire. She had no idea a broken nose could hurt so much. Fresh tears sprang into her eyes. She could smell oil, and less strong, gasoline. If she lit the matches she might catch the trunk on fire. Was that a possibility? She didn't know. But if she didn't drive the darkness away what would happen? Would the thing in the dark inhabit her body and protect her, kill Blake? Or was that simply a fantasy? Would she just hyperventilate and pass out? What was the truth? Was she the killer, or was Blake? If it was Blake then she wanted to live, but if it wasn't, if the thing truly was inside her, then maybe Blake was doing her a favor. She had to have time to think, to figure it all out.

She struck the first match. It sputtered but caught. It was so lovely. She watched its blue and yellow flame as it leapt and danced in response to the sway of the car. The smell of sulfur was strong in the small enclosed space.

Why had he done it? Had he killed Bunny and Janice and attacked Muncie? What possible reason could he have to hate her so much? What did he have against the others?

The match burned her fingers and, fearful of dropping it onto the oil-soaked carpeting, Austin blew it out and awkwardly struck another.

That was a mistake, she realized. You have to wait until you begin to fear the dark, the something in the dark, before you use them. You can't afford to run out. But for the moment she let herself enjoy the feeble light.

The trip took 16 matches. Only four were left when the car pulled onto gravel, slowed and stopped. She was ready.

She heard him open the door. The car rose as he

climbed out. She heard the driver's door close and his footsteps on the gravel. She heard the key slide into the lock without fumbling or hesitation and wondered if he had been drunk at all.

He swung the lid up. The smoke from the matches, which had been hovering near the top of the trunk, drifted out. It took Blake's attention for just one moment, but that moment was long enough. Austin drew the razor sharp blade of the box knife across the back of his hand.

She'd been carrying the knife ever since the night in the nursery, when Will had walked in on her. She'd forgotten about it until, when fumbling for the matches, she'd found it in her pocket.

Blake shrieked in pain, cupping his hand and stepping back as the knife sliced through his skin. Austin swung her legs out of the trunk and sprang to her feet in one smooth movement.

Night had fallen since they'd left the house, but the full moon was up and the snow reflected the light, revealing Blake's face. His anger was frightening, his eyes rolling and mad.

"Stay away from me," she warned, brandishing the knife. He stepped back, and keeping his eyes on her he pulled the scarf from his neck and began to wind it around his injured hand. Blood had fallen in dark splatters against the pristine snow. Taking one step back, then another, then turning, she ran. The snow crunched beneath her feet. It was cold. Her breath streamed behind her in a ragged scarf. The moonlight was strong, but cloud shadows made the ground tricky to navigate. She could hear him behind her, so close, so very close, and then she couldn't hear his running footsteps any more. But she didn't dare look back. She had to concentrate, had to run. She could outrun him.

She had to believe that.

Then she heard the car. He had gone back for the car. She was at the road now, running alongside the ditch knowing she would have to cross it and get to the other side. Why did the chicken cross the road? To keep from getting run over by the bastard in the rented car and the ten-gallon hat, she thought insanely. The car kept coming, fast and loud. He wouldn't dare the ditch would he? She gathered herself and leapt. She hit the opposite side of the bank hard and slid downward, one foot smashing through a crust of ice, water filling her shoe. She clawed at the frozen ground and pulled herself up to the top of the ditch.

She could hear the tires crunching across the snow and the tick of a bad lifter in the engine. Getting to her feet, she half ran, half stumbled away, using the ditch as a guide and staying just below the darkest shadows cast by the line of trees on the hillside.

Her breath was ragged and a stitch burned in her side, rivaling the throbbing ache of her broken nose. The lights of the car swept across her, and she imagined she could feel its heat, like some modern dragon breathing down her neck, growing closer and closer. Knowing she had to make up her mind to either run into the darkness of the forest or give up all chance of getting away, Austin turned to climb. Then a new sound took her attention. She turned in time to see the car sliding sideways alongside the ditch. She could hear tires skidding over the slick sheet ice and then the car abruptly went into the ditch. It struck the side hard, flinging frozen clods of mud as it flipped onto its back and continued sliding. She watched, awestruck, as it seemed to pick up speed and then suddenly stopped. It sat rocking, tires spinning, headlights shining uselessly at the base of pine and fir.

Austin didn't know how long she stood there. Finally she became aware of how quiet the night had become. There was an utter stillness, broken only by the pinging of the cooling engine, a metallic cricket, chirping without rhythm.

"Austin."

She heard her name, and her hand tightened on the box knife she had clutched the whole time.

"Help me. Please, Austin. I'm hurt bad."

He doesn't sound drunk at all. He's a trickster, a liar. Why believe him now?

"Austin, please."

She didn't know how many times he called her name before she made up her mind and resignedly made her way to the car. Kneeling in the snow, she could look inside the window of the upside down car. In her current state of mind she had lost touch with much of the world, sliding through a grayness that was part shock, but she had not yet lost touch with the basic humanity that says you do not leave the injured to die alone.

What she saw did not touch her, though it would make a rookie paramedic throw up his dinner later that night.

It took her a few moments to puzzle out what she was seeing, to understand the strange weapon that the universe had provided for her. The thick branch of a spruce tree had broken under the weight of last year's storms and fallen into the crotch of another tree where it sat like a bolt in a crossbow; loaded, aimed, and waiting.

But it was the car that had provided the momentum to slam the sharpened end of the branch through the fractured driver's side window as it slid sideways toward the target. It was the car's momentum that had forced the spike of a branch to pierce Blake's body below his left armpit, through his body and out between the shattered ribs on his right side. He was pinned like an insect to the seat of the car. Austin stood beside him and heard him take his last breath.

After a few moments Austin stood, then she walked eight miles to the nearest house with a light on. Given her broken nose, twisted ankle and badly torn knee that she could walk at all was something of a miracle. Frostbite took a bite from her ankle and darkened her toes but they recovered fully with time.

Townspeople compared her walk to the amazing stories of people who lift cars from trapped children. They did not understand the strength she drew upon came, not from adrenaline, but from the relief of knowing it was Blake and not she who had committed the murders.

The story came to light gradually. The man calling himself Blake had been Muncie's friend Brian. He had known them for a little more than a year. The time they had lived in Germany.

"Blake, or actually Brian, was the product of a seriously disturbed family," Mark explained to Austin, as they sat in his office two days after a Christmas she had not felt like celebrating.

"I have a friend on the police force who told me what he knows, with the promise I'd only use the information to help in your therapy. I do have to ask you not to discuss this with anyone else until the story comes out to the public."

"Of course," agreed Austin. "Tell me what you know."

"Well first, the police found a journal in Brian's room that mentions how he believed you destroyed his happiness the day you got locked in that bomb shelter. Apparently, your mother was pretty upset about the incident and she spoke to Brian's mother about his part in it. Brian's mother then spoke to her husband.

She must have confronted him, possibly blamed him for Brian's behavior. We will probably never know what set him off. According to old medical records, the wife had been physically abused for years. This time the abuse got out of hand. She fell -- or, more accurately, was pushed -- down a flight of stairs. She died from her injuries. There was a court martial, and Brian's father was convicted of second-degree murder and sent to prison.

Brian was sent to live with grandparents but they couldn't handle him. He ended up in a series of foster homes and residential treatment facilities for alcoholism.

Somehow he became obsessed with the idea that you had purposely overreacted to the short time you were in the shelter. He thinks you faked the trauma to get attention, which caused his parents to argue and inevitably were the reason his family fell apart."

Austin sat back in her chair and sighed. "In a way I can almost feel sorry for him. I can see how he twisted things up and hated me, but I don't get why he didn't come directly after me. Why go after my family and friends instead? It seems like such a lot of work, not to mention complexity. Also, I'm not sure why he didn't find me earlier? What took so long?"

"If I were to guess, I'd say that he has been heading in this direction, figuratively that is, for some time. It was probably some new catalyst, a trauma of some sort that set him in motion literally. Or maybe it was as simple as his finding out where you were. Your name is unusual for a woman. How hard would it be to find an Austin Ward, female? You own a business. You probably pop up on web searches."

"I suppose so," Austin agreed.

"So he decides to find you and punish you for what he thinks is his ruined life," Mark continued. "He learns you're afraid of the dark. Maybe he's known that since Germany."

"Which should have shown him I wasn't acting afraid, I really was afraid. I was only seven years old," Austin complained, railing against the injustice of it, the waste of three lives.

"Brian's father died in prison 16 months ago. I imagine that may have been what set him searching for you. There is no logic to it. You can't apply normal thinking to his behavior. We may never know why people like Brian become so…" The ringing phone interrupted him. Mark walked to the desk to pick it up. "Sorry," he said to her. "I usually turn the phone off, but I'm expecting a call. "Yes. Thank you," he said into the phone, then after a few moments, "Yes, I'll do that." He hung up, then sat back down across from Austin and took her hand. "One last shock. It'll be in the papers, so you should know."

"Yes?"

"The police have been searching for the box Brian talked about. They found it."

"It was real?" she asked.

"Buried near that fishing spot on the river. Don't know how he pulled it off, but. . ."

Austin moved across the space between them. She had been brave, had been calm and used her intelligence to escape Brian and his plans for her, but the reality of what he had meant to do to her, the idea of being buried alive in a dark box deep in the ground stripped her of her last defenses. Moving into Mark's arms, trusting she would find a refuge there, she closed her eyes and thanked God it was over.

Five days after Christmas, Mark knocked on Austin's door. When she opened it she was surprised by a flurry of soft fur and huge feet as a puppy wobbled through the door and clumsily ran into her legs. She knelt down and the puppy yipped happily, licking her and panting puppy breath in her face. She laughed and looked up at Mark.

"Merry Christmas," he said.

"Mine?"

"Well, you told me you didn't have time for a dog, so I thought maybe we could work out a time-share. You interested in half a dog?"

"Ok. But I want the good end."

"You can have a side, left or right. That's the deal," Mark insisted.

"Fine, I'll take the left," she said, stroking the pup's soft fur.

"The heart side. Figures," said Mark with a grin.

Chapter 34

In the spring, when the ice melted and the runoff from the mountains swept through the culvert in Austin's driveway, they found Josh. It was the meter reader who spotted the bones as the churning waters pushed them through the grating meant to filter out debris.

There was nothing Austin could do with this new, but not unexpected, news. Tears were never enough. She had learned that lesson in the past year. They could never wash away all the pain of loss.

Mark was there. Muncie was there. She had to keep reminding herself that she was not completely alone.

It was the last and possibly the hardest in a series of blows from which Austin felt she would never fully recover. She stopped for a pack of cigarettes and drove to the river. It was still her favorite place, though she avoided the patch of ground near the edge of the woods where she'd learned that Blake had buried a wooden shipping crate. It was as if that piece of earth was poisoned. She avoided even looking at it.

Spring was coming. She had told Blake that Spruce had

only two seasons, but that hadn't been entirely true. Spring, whether it lasted a month or a day, was still a promise carried by the rushing rivers and greening hills, the rising sap and soaring spirits. Austin wondered if she would ever feel that sense of elation, of any good emotion, again. The darkness of Granny's dream and of Blake's plan, the darkness of the hole-in-the-wall all seemed to have seeped from their confinement and filled the world, or at least her world.

She walked to the edge of the river. The old fisherman was just pushing off in his boat and nodded a hello to her before paddling toward his favorite spot below the bridge. Waving, she stepped onto the dock. It creaked as always, moving more loosely now that the ice had melted from its edges, though it did still rime the boards, a reminder that winter had not yet fully loosened its grasp.

She opened the pack of cigarettes and lit up. The smoke was harsh and she coughed on the first few inhalations. It was a strange tribute, she realized: a cigarette to celebrate the life of someone who hadn't had time to really live. The smoke burned her throat. Standing there, she let herself remember Josh's wry wit, his sense of responsibility, and that small streak of rebelliousness. She thought he might have grown up to be a good man. Tossing the butt of her cigarette into the river, she lit another. The sun was warm on her shoulders. She took off her parka, laid it on the dock and sat cross-legged on it. The heavy sweater she'd worn under the parka was just enough to keep off the worst of the chill.

The sun was dull, burning behind a drift of gray clouds. The water was the color of dirty bronze, a still mirror of the sky. Austin took another drag, then felt the shift as someone stepped onto the dock.

"Austin."

Turning, she recognized Muncie. "Did you come to take me back home? I'm fine."

"You're not fine and we both know it."

"Some things you can't fix, big brother."

"I know. I've known a long time."

"What do you mean?"

"About you. About the something in the dark that you told me about, back when we were kids. I know how it possesses you. How you…do things."

"What do you mean?" she asked. Muncie stepped forward and knelt beside her.

"You must suspect. You must know that it wasn't all Brian. It couldn't have been."

"Are you saying?"

"It was you who attacked me, Austin. I turned just enough when you swung that second time. I saw you."

"But Will? You said it was Will."

"You're my sister. I have to take care of you. Dad and Mom both asked me to take care of you. They both knew. We all did, but you were ours, and we had to…"

"Take care of me."

"It didn't happen every time. I don't think it happened every time you got scared, just some of the time. Enough to make us worry. We taught you to keep a source of light around.

"To protect myself."

"To protect us."

"I did things? Bad things?"

"When we were little. When you were nine. I found

you in the garage with our dog. You had locked yourself in somehow and hid the key. We didn't even know you were there, but the poor dog."

"You told me she got hit by a car."

"That was because you came out of it and you saw, and how else could we explain?"

"My God, Muncie, what kind of monster am I? I think I suspected…I knew something was wrong with me. Things kept happening: dried blood on my hands. I could have killed you and the others. Was Bunny? Did Brian kill Bunny or was it…?"

He didn't answer, but his silence was answer enough.

"It's my hands with blood on them. My hands holding the hammer and the pipe and the God knows what else. Quit protecting me. Tell me all of it. I have to know."

"I think you must have killed Janice," Muncie admitted in a near whisper. "I think Bunny too. I don't know about Josh, but what reason would Blake have had? He may have been insanely determined to punish you, but why the others? There would be no reason. He just took responsibility for it, bragged about it, to scare you."

"It worked."

"I know. But you don't have to be scared any more. He's dead too. They all are."

"That's what happens isn't it? Every time someone gets close to me. Every time I care about someone they disappear. They die."

"Not all of them. I'm still here."

"Only by the grace of God and my poor aim."

Muncie stood, then leaned over and kissed the top of Austin's head. He stroked her hair gently and said, "We will get through this. Now that you know everything, we will fix it. Go home soon. It's getting late. I have to go now." Austin watched him walk slowly to his truck, climb in with the weariness of an old man, and drive away.

She sat staring deeply into the water. It was cold down there, cold and quiet as a tomb. Down there, no one was waiting to die. Before she could change her mind, before the evil that could possess her had one more chance, she dove. The water closed around her and bubbles of air burst from her clothing and foamed to the surface. It was cold. So cold the shock was like burning. She wanted heat, warmth. She fought the urge to swim. She grasped her arms and began to sink. As she slid away from the sun, as her feet touched the floor of the river, the darkness closed around her. The fear that had been part of her for so long clawed free from the primitive part of her brain and it was that instinct alone that took over, forcing her to fight and claw for the light.

Breaking to the surface, she took a deep breath of air into her aching lungs. She had no idea which direction to swim. The cold was cramping her legs and arms. She knew she had only moments left, but she felt neither grateful nor afraid. All she could feel was the burn of the water she had gasped into her lungs, the pain shooting through her chest.

Then she felt something smack the water beside her. She grabbed for it instinctively, and her hand closed weakly around the paddle end of an oar. The old fisherman pulled her slowly toward his boat until she could hook her arm over its side while he paddled both of them to shore.

An hour later, with the help of her truck's heater and several cups of gin-laced coffee, she finally stopped shivering.

"You think you're feeling good enough to drive home

now?"

"Yes, I think so," she told him softly, her voice hoarse from the river water and the harsh gin.

"You sure give me a start. Them boards is slippery and you was sure lucky someone was around to pull you out when you fell in."

"I sure was."

"Good thing, too. I spotted that fella you was talking to. Was gonna head to the other side of the bridge, but once I recognized him, I thought I'd hang around see what he was up to this time.."

"What do you mean?"

"Well that fella's some entertaining. He's got himself a great big 'ol Cat. He was out here some time ago digging a hole in the ground. 'Round there, back in them trees," he said, pointing to the spot that Austin thought of as poisoned ground.

"I always wanted to run one of them big Cats. Heavy equipment operator's what I always wanted to be, so when I seen him running that thing I had to hang 'round and watch. Imagine he was fixing a sewer line or something, but it sure was pretty the way he could dig a hole in that hard frozen ground just like that. He snapped his fingers and nodded. His dark eyes sparkled with the memory. Austin noted the deep wrinkles around his eyes, the tangled gray beard and liver-spotted head and wondered how much she could trust his memory.

"Are you sure it was him?"

"Sure as I am it was you fell in the water. Seen him a few times 'round here. Wears red mostly, and that yellow jacket with the patch of duct tape on the pocket. Sews pretty much as good as I do, I'd guess."

"I have to go now," Austin said. "Thank you. I never realized how awkward it would be to say thank you to someone for saving my life."

"No stranger than my saying you're welcome, I suppose. You get home and get into a hot bath and then some dry clothes. You sure you ain't had too much of that gin to drive?"

"I'd say I had just the right amount. And thank you for that, too."

"Well, you are welcome again." He climbed out of the truck slowly, feeling for the running board gingerly but once he was firmly on the ground his stride was quick and sure. Austin drove from the parking lot slowly, careful of black ice, but she had no intention of going home.

Chapter 35

Her nearly dry, badly tangled hair kept getting in her eyes, and she brushed it back with shaking fingers. Her clothes were damp and she looked as wild as she felt as she drove to The Lake House.

When she pulled up the driveway she was not at all surprised to see Muncie sitting on a lawn chair at the end of the private dock, his back to her. He had not turned when she pulled in, or when he heard her walking toward him. He knew who it was and he was simply waiting.

As she stepped onto the dock and took in his relaxed slouch, his wide shoulders, she realized she was no longer as sure of herself. Muncie was strong, with muscles honed by years of operating hand tools and hauling lumber. Physically, she was in good shape too, but she was no match for him and she knew it.

Initially, armed with the truth about her friends' deaths and freed from guilt and self-doubt, she had felt invincible. Now, she realized, she was not operating with anything approximating reason or logic. Her friends would have suggested she call the police. Leave it all to them. In fact, it occurred to her, as she walked steadily toward Muncie, that she had been operating on some kind of autopilot since her leap into the river. That she had no idea what she was going to do, no weapon to use against him. All she really had were a whole lot of questions.

"Beer?" he asked fishing one out of the small cooler next to him, holding it up, still without bothering to turn to look at her. This only added to the general "Through The Looking Glass" aspect of the afternoon.

"No thanks," she said stopping short of the dock. "Got a cigarette? I got mine all wet."

"Sorry. You know I never took up the habit. I'm kind of surprised that you're smoking again. It's not a good thing, you know."

"Really? Do you really care?"

"Such anger," Muncie chided.

"I have reason."

"I suppose." He opened the can of beer he'd offered her and took a long drink.

"Turn around," Austin said, "I don't want to talk to your back."

With a long-suffering sigh, he stood, turned the lawn chair to face her, and sat back down.

"So, didn't fall for it, I see."

"Oh, but I did. I'm pretty stupid, you know."

"Yes. You never were as smart as you thought."

"Probably true."

"No probably about it," he said, smirking.

"How did you make it all work?"

"Why should I tell you?"

"Because I'm intrigued by your brilliance, and you like that."

"I know you think you're being funny, but maybe you're closer to the truth than you know. I am a genius, after all. Or did you forget that? The tests all said so. Our folks were proud of me once. They thought I'd be a doctor and discover a cure for some horrible disease. That's what geniuses do, after all. He tossed his empty beer can into the cooler.

"At least, they thought I was pretty great until…well, I'm sure you remember when."

Austin shook her head.

"Come on now. It was right after you had your little dramatic moment. After that they had to spend all their time taking care of you, dealing with your emotional issues. Couldn't be left alone. Couldn't be in the dark. Be nice to your sister. Don't pick on your sister. Don't scare your sister. Remember the whipping I got that time I unscrewed the light bulbs and locked you in your room?"

"I don't remember."

"Typical. You don't remember much, do you?"

His voice was getting shrill, spitting words as much as saying them. She barely recognized the brother she loved under all that rage.

"It's always been the best part of the game," he said, his voice growing soft now, a smile pulling at the corners of his mouth.

"Tell me about the game." Austin asked softly.

"Oh, he said with a chuckle, "the game. You know about the game. On some level you must. How many times were you so afraid that you blacked out and then when you woke up everything had changed, you were in a different room, you were in different clothes. Seeing your face, watching you try to pretend nothing was wrong. That was priceless. At first, making the arrangements to scare you was the best part of the game. Then finding out that once you blacked out I could control you, make you move around, sit down, lie down, and never remember a single thing that was when the real fun began. Once," Muncie covered his mouth and giggled. "Once, I took your panties off and threw them in the garbage. I waited to see if you'd say anything when you came out of it but you never said a word."

Austin sensed that Muncie was hoping she would react. He wanted her angry, upset. He wanted to manipulate her emotions as easily as he had her body. She refused to give him what he wanted. She refused to show how deeply disgusted she was that her own brother had looked at her, had undressed her, maybe even touched her, how many times?

"Don't go getting weird ideas," he said, and she realized something must have conveyed her thoughts. "There was no sexual stuff going on. You're my sister, remember. And I'm no freaking pervert."

"I didn't say you were. I just don't get it. I don't understand the game. I don't understand where Brian came from. It's a huge…"

"Oh, Brian. That was a new twist. I never expected that. He did come looking for us. Your friend Mark was right about that. He was even right about how he found us, but Muncie is a much more unusual name than Austin. He found me first."

Austin didn't know what bothered her most, Muncie's cold arrogance or his years of deception. She wanted to scream, to throw and hit and let loose her anger. She held it all back. She had to hear this, had to know all of it.

"Once he told me who he was," Muncie continued, "and why he was so pissed off, it was easy to convince him you were the problem. I told him you'd ruined my life too, just like you'd ruined his. A few months feeding his drinking habit, stroking his ego, and letting him fall in love with me, and he would have done anything to you I suggested."

Austin winced at Muncie's gleeful laughter. The way he reveled in her pain as he made one horrific revelation after another made the depth of his mental illness frighteningly clear.

"Of course winding up a shish kabob was his own fault. People never listen. I told him how to take care of you. A few minutes in a dark trunk and you'd be out of it. He wanted to sleep with you. Actually he wanted to fuck your brains out. Not because he wanted you of course, but because it would have been sort of like being with me, which is what he really wanted.

I promised him that he could do anything he wanted to you as long as he didn't kill you before he put you in the hole. You had to be alive, and I was hoping conscious, when he locked you in. I knew that would be the only way to find out what would happen if I kept you in a dark place for a really long time. I've always wondered about that. Would you eventually have woken up, or would you have stayed lost in that place you go, forever?

"Good old scientific curiosity?" she asked, her voice dripping with sarcasm and disgust.

"Why not," he said ignoring her tone. "I never had the nerve to find out before because I was afraid it would mess everything up, end the game. Well, the game was over. You wanted me to move away to Portland. You were pushing and pushing to end the game. Fine," he snapped. "So I had Brian put a microphone in the box and set it to record whenever there was noise. I figured I'd dig you up after a couple weeks and retrieve the tape and that would tell me if you ever came back out of it. Pretty clever, right?"

"The night I got locked in the potting shed, was that the night it started?" Austin asked. She could feel her entire body trembling, not just from cold but from the waves of emotion that were crashing through her body, eroding her strength.

"Sure. I knew Bunny wasn't coming in 'cause I'd made a date to meet her that night. I even talked her into calling and pretending she was coming down with something. After a little romp in the sack I asked her to come to the nursery with me. She told me about getting it on with your hired hand. That really pissed me off," Muncie explained. "Here she was getting the best and she goes and gets knocked up, or so she thinks, by the village idiot. Then she has the audacity to complain to me about it. That's when I started thinking it was time to teach the little bitch a lesson.

After I killed her I heard you in the shed singing. That's when I got the idea to shut the door, drop the bar and cut the power. After a few minutes I rescued you." He laughed, amused by his own cleverness.

"But why?" Austin asked.

"Why?" What do you mean why? All you talk about lately is wanting me to leave. I decided it was . . . well maybe it was the right time for the game to change.

"But I have this thing about prison. I thought about it a lot and with you wanting me to leave and all...well, maybe it was the right time for the game to change. When I thought about how much fun it would be to take care of the bitch and then set things up to convince you that you had done it. Now come on, you have to admit that was inspired."

"You are a total bastard and completely crazy," Austin sputtered.

"Stop being such a sister. I want to tell you the rest of it. See the really tricky part was getting Brian sober enough to shut off the power to your house at just the right time and then to wake you up. You running into the door and getting the black eye was bonus points. Very nice."

"And Janice?"

"Janice wanted to tell you about us. She thought we were in love, but I convinced her you were too fragile to deal with the idea of her moving to Portland with me. She bought that one for a while, but then she got insistent and, well, you know how it goes. I always knew I'd eventually have to get rid of her. I didn't want you to find out I was sleeping with her. It might look bad if every female I'm boning dies tragically, right?"

Austin felt locked in place, her feet planted on the narrow strip of grass at the edge of the dock. The waves rolling slowly across the lake were making her feel dizzy, and she swayed.

"No passing out, damn it. Enough of that. I haven't even told you about Josh yet. I had just finished with Janice, and I was walking across the school grounds and toward my truck, which I'd cleverly parked a few blocks away, and I almost walked into him.

"Kid was all over the place on that bike. Probably out scoring some weed or something, but I realized he'd seen me and that was not good. Once he found out about Janice, he'd start to wonder what I was doing there and maybe he'd figure it out. So being a nice guy, I offered him a ride home, and he took me up on it. I put his bike in the back but told him I had to stop at your place because you thought you'd forgot to lock the front door.

"I got out and walked up to the porch and he got out to catch a smoke. I didn't even have to trick him out of the truck. I picked up one of those obsidian rocks you have bordering the flower bed in your front yard. I fiddled with the front door, made some comment about sisters and what a pain in the ass they were. Then I walked up on him and hit him in the head a couple of times."

Austin shuddered. His words tore through her colder than any wind.

"He was pretty hard-headed though, Muncie continued. "and just wouldn't go down. He tried to grab ahold of me and I ended up having to wrestle him to the ditch and stick his face in the water and hold him under for awhile. Afterwards I shoved him in the culvert and pinned him there with his bike. I figured by the time he broke loose the water would have washed off any evidence I'd left behind."

The police had taken Austin's box knife long ago, and she had no other weapon, but she launched herself at him. Surprised by her sudden rush, Muncie scrambled to his feet but stumbled over the cooler. They fell into the water together. Muncie struggled to swim to the surface, while Austin concentrated on holding him under. Her only fear was that she would give out first and die before she could drown him.

He managed to push her away and reach the dock pulling himself up until his forearms were resting on the surface, pausing to catch his breath. She lunged out of the water, grabbed a handful of his hair, and pulled him back under. They swirled through the water, sinking fast. He tried to push her away, but she clung to him with arms and legs and teeth. The second time he managed to reach the surface he gasped out, "I've got Mark. He's not dead yet, but…"

"Liar." Gasping, she bit down hard on his ear and dug her fingers into the soft skin under his jaw. He slid back under the water but only for a moment. With a burst of strength he managed to kick toward the dock, reach up to grab the edge and pull both of them out of the water. Bright red and white stars exploded in front of her eyes as he swung an elbow that clipped her on the side of the head, and she fell back in, swallowing a cup of lake water.

This time, as he tried to pull himself onto the dock, she didn't try to stop him. Coughing, half-choking, she paddled to shore and climbed out. Her second dunking in icy water had drained her and left her shivering from head to foot.

"Where's Mark?" she croaked.

"Help me," Muncie demanded through clenched teeth.

With her sodden jeans like iron weights around her legs, Austin staggered to the end of the dock, took hold of a handful of Muncie's shirt and pulled him along the side until he reached shallow water and was able to stand.

"W-w-w-where?"

"Get warm first," Muncie said. He stumbled toward the house, water streaming from his clothes. Knowing he had the upper hand, Austin decided to go along, at least for the moment. Besides, her teeth were chattering and she knew if she didn't get warm and dry soon, she wouldn't be able to put up any kind of fight. She stripped to her bra and panties, feeling too vulnerable to be naked, and climbed into the shower. The hot water felt like a second chance, taking the chill from her fingers so that she could flex them again. When she was thoroughly warm, she stepped from the shower, dried off as best she could and slipped into Muncie's old yellow jacket. Luckily it was long and reached nearly to her knees.

Muncie came out the bathroom wearing a set of painters' coveralls he'd left on the job.

"Where is he?" Austin demanded.

"A box buried somewhere. You know how I like burying things."

"Bullshit. The police filled it in."

"Sure, they buried the one by the river, but I built two." He held up two fingers. "And they both have microphones."

"You sick fucking bastard."

"Now Austin. You know it's not polite to use that kind of language. I'm afraid you've been naughty and will have to be punished."

With the full revelation of her brother's insanity and increasingly aware that he was beyond reasoning, Austin felt sick and lightheaded. All she could think about was how she wanted him dead, the way you'd want a rabid dog dead, so it couldn't bite anyone. But she had to be careful. Sometimes it felt like she was speaking to her brother, sometimes it felt like she was speaking to a demented and very naughty child.

If Mark really was where Muncie said, if he were buried out there, then chances were no one would find him. He would die alone and in darkness. She had to trick Muncie into believing she was willing to play along. She had to learn where the box, and Mark, were buried. "You have to take me to him." She pleaded. "If you do that I'll go with you somewhere. We can keep playing the game."

"I don't believe you."

240

"What choice do I have?" she reasoned with him.

"You tried to kill me."

"Oh, I did not, you big baby. I was just playing with you. I know how much you've helped me all these years. Where would I be without you? I was kind of mad about your dumb game, but you don't really think I'd try to kill you. You're my brother."

"That's right," Muncie finally said, with a grin. "I guess it was fair play. But if you really want to save Mark you have to do one more thing to even things up."

"What?"

He walked out into the driveway and Austin followed him. He gestured toward his truck. "Get in the box. That's how I'll take you to him."

"Go to hell."

"Get in the box or leave Mark in his. Show me you trust me, that you really aren't still mad about the game and I'll take you to him. Make up your mind."

Austin looked toward the lake. The sun was going down, the fading light leaving dancing sparkles on the water that stung her eyes.

"Look, your friend is running out of time. If you run away and go to the cops you'll never figure out where the box is in time. He's already running out of air. So quit fooling around and get in the box."

Austin moved her gaze to the back of Muncie's pickup. Her pulse quickened. The oversized metal toolbox would hold her. There was no pretending it wouldn't. Muncie took his keys out of the cab of the truck and climbed over the tailgate into the bed. He unlocked the toolbox and began unloading it, setting tools and tool bags into the bed of the truck.

"I don't know that I should trust you, Muncie," Austin admitted. "How do I know you won't just bury me along with Mark?"

"Because then the game would be over and I've decided I don't want it to be.

"How nice for you."

"Quit trying to make me mad, you're just stalling. Get in the box."

Reluctantly, Austin obeyed. She climbed into the bed of the truck and stepped into the chromed steel toolbox.

The only way she could fit was to lay on her side with her knees drawn up.

"Now I know you think I'm a monster, but I'm really a very nice brother, see?" Muncie handed Austin a flashlight. She took it with both her hands, gratefully. As he swung the lid of the box shut she pressed the switch on the flashlight. Nothing happened.

"I said I'd give you a flashlight," Muncie said, laughing maliciously. "I didn't say I'd put batteries in it. Nighty night, Sis. Oh, and by the way, I don't know where the hell Mark is. Of course there was only one hole. Why would I need two? I can't believe you fell for that. I am disappointed, little sister."

Austin lay still, clutching the useless flashlight. The darkness seemed to pulse around her. The sounds her brother made were growing distant and unimportant. She realized she was tired and not completely unhappy with this new twist in the game. Like an old woman whose friends and family have all gone on ahead, she felt ready. She had made peace with her mortality the moment before she jumped into the water at the fishing hole.

Then a thought occurred to her. Had Muncie been

lying when he said he had Mark, or was this new declaration the lie? What if Mark *was* buried in the ground, trapped in a small narrow place, just like this one, unable to see, unable to breathe?

She had wanted to surrender to the darkness, to give up and slip into the familiar territory of her personal nightmare. There was a certainty that Muncie would not let her live to play the game as he'd promised. They both knew that the game had ended the instant she learned of its existence.

After enough time had gone by, Muncie took a crescent wrench from the bed of the truck, and holding it upraised in his right hand, carefully lifted the lid of the box with his left. He found his sister curled up in the same position she'd been in when he closed the box an hour earlier. The worthless flashlight he'd given her lay between her feet where she'd dropped it. He set the wrench down and reached to take her arm, to help her climb out of the box on his command.

She struck suddenly, slashing at his face. A bead of red pearls appeared across his neck, and there was a stinging sensation. He put his hand to his throat and felt warm liquid spurt between his fingers. He lurched back a step, keeping his hand pressed hard against the gaping wound.

"What did you do?" he asked, his voice quivering. Then, petulantly, "Why are you conscious?"

"Because I decided not to be afraid anymore," she spat. "Because I'm sick and tired of your game. I don't want to play any more. Is Mark buried or not? Did you lie? Where is he?"

"I don't know. I don't care. Why are you so worried about him? What about me? Look at me. Look what you did." Blood continued to seep from behind his fingers and run in rivulets, staining the front of his coveralls.

Austin climbed out of the box. The broken shard of the flashlight's lens was still in her hand, caught in the fold of the duct tape she'd peeled from his jacket and wound around her fingers to protect them. She moved to the edge of the truck, sat down and swung her legs over, then dropped to the ground.

"Where are you going?" Muncie demanded. "Are you going to get help?"

Austin backed away.

Muncie climbed over the tailgate. He kept his right hand pressed against the wound on his neck and used his left to brace himself as he used the rear bumper as a step. His knees buckled when his feet touched the ground, but he clung to the side of the truck and didn't fall.

His attention, which had been on Austin, swung away to the lake, and he let go of the truck and staggered toward the dock.

When he stepped onto the dock it swayed. He lost his balance and fell to his knees.

Austin ran to the dock and knelt beside him. "Please, tell me where Mark is."

"I don't know," Muncie said. He was never part of it."

"You lied?" Austin asked.

"I always liked it here," Muncie said, ignoring the question. "I drug the job out as much as I could." He began to slump. Austin pulled him against her and put his head in her lap. "I liked the game. I wish we could have played it just a little longer."

"Me too," Austin said, pushing the damp hair out of his eyes, stroking his face.

"I didn't really want to kill you," he said.

"It wasn't you," Austin told him. "It was that thing— that whatever it was we found in the dark. It got inside all of us. You. Me. Brian."

"Hmmm," said Muncie, sleepily.

The moon rose and by its light Austin could see Muncie's blood, a black stain across her fingers.

"You never really played the game, Austin. Not like me and Brian. You never did anything bad at all." His hand fell away from his neck, but it didn't matter. The blood had stopped.

"Of course I did, Muncie," said Austin. "I killed you."

Across the bowl of the sky the stars came out.

Pamela Cowan

ABOUT THE AUTHOR

Pamela Cowan writes mystery and suspense thrillers. Her short fiction has been published in various magazines and read on radio. Cowan has worked as an audio producer, a magazine editor, and in the probation and parole side of criminal justice. Like Austin, she once owned a landscaping business in Southern Oregon.

She now lives with her husband and a number of four-legged roommates near Portland, Oregon where she is currently working on her fourth novel, *Cold Kill*.

Visit her website @ pamelacowan.com and sign up for the quarterly giveaway or the Kill Your Colleague Contest!

Pamela Cowan

Dear Reader,

As an independent author I don't have the marketing engine of a large publishing company behind me. What I do have is readers such as yourself who are willing to leave a review on Amazon.com. So, if you enjoyed this book please consider taking a moment to leave a review.

Thank you very much,
Pamela Cowan

Pamela Cowan

Made in the USA
Coppell, TX
06 August 2022

81037354R00144